The Gun-Master of Saddleback

Center Point
Large Print

Also by D. B. Newton and available from
Center Point Large Print:

Bounty on Bannister
Bullets on the Wind
Syndicate Gun
Broken Spur
Fury at Three Forks
Range Boss
Trail of the Bear

The Gun-Master of Saddleback

D. B. NEWTON

CENTER POINT LARGE PRINT
THORNDIKE, MAINE

This Center Point Large Print edition
is published in the year 2024 by arrangement with
Golden West Inc.

Copyright © 1948 by Phoenix Press.

All rights reserved.

First US edition: Phoenix Press
First UK edition: Sampson Low

The text of this Large Print edition is unabridged.
In other aspects, this book may vary
from the original edition.
Printed in the United States of America
on permanent paper sourced using
environmentally responsible foresting methods.
Set in 16-point Times New Roman type.

ISBN 979-8-89164-211-9 (hardcover)
ISBN 979-8-89164-215-7 (paperback)

The Library of Congress has cataloged this record
under Library of Congress Control Number: 2024933838

CHAPTER I

The big man said: "Right here's where the wind swats you a regular wallop!"

He was already leaning forward a little as he said it, bracing himself expectantly; now the plodding of the bay mare lifted him into the stream of air that whipped through the gap, and the words were plucked from his lips half-uttered and hurled away across thick, bent shoulders.

Behind him there was a smothered curse, and hipping around in saddle Ross Boyden let a grin touch his broad, flat-lipped mouth, while the red checked shirt snapped and fluttered at his wide chest. Back there, the new man had been forming a smoke as he jogged into the gap, and now the fingers of the wind had torn the paper from his hands, slapped the shredded tobacco against his face in a stinging cloud. The new man ducked, pawing at his eyes. He spat grain tobacco from his lips and swiped the back of a hand across them. The hand was lean and freckled, and covered with a matting of fine blond hair.

The new man cursed again. "Thanks for the warning!" he growled.

Boyden laughed at him. "You're high when you've got this far, and there's nothin' at all to stop her once the old breeze starts whooshing across the ridge. Now we're comin' up to the Saddle—that's what they call this pass connecting the east slope and the west." They had drawn into the protection of a twisted clump of swaying, battered juniper. The big man reined his mount around and pointed. "Look. You can see the way we been."

The new man, intent on learning fast the layout of this country where he had found hire for himself and his gun, spat out the last of the tobacco crumbs and turned to follow Boyden's gesture. He was mildly surprised. This trail up the eastern skirt of the Saddle took the grade so easily he hadn't been aware how steeply the land dropped away below.

Dry range was down there, browning now in the fierce summer heat. It was fair graze, but it needed water and there was none. Only the dry courses where, not long before, streams and springs had flowed—mere white streaks of sand now. Lifting his head, the new man squinted up at old Baldy's crest where the big mountain showed, high and asparkle, in cold splendour against the blue. "Where's this slide," he demanded suddenly, "that's causing all the trouble?"

Ross Boyden waved a broad, fleshy hand vaguely upward. "Yonderly," he answered. "It'd be hard to get to."

They put their horses out again into the channel of the wind, and they had it to their faces as they pushed on through the notch. But when they came out of the gap—out upon the wide back of the saddle itself—the hard hand of the wind was lifted from them abruptly. Its going left a humming in their ears and a whipped numbness in reddened faces.

"You can go ahead and build that quirly now," said Boyden. "It ain't so bad up here—wind just seems to collect somehow and go whistlin' through that notch." But the new man had forgotten about his smoke by this time.

They rode for a while in silence. The pass was appropriately named. Wide and deep, the Saddle's pommel and cantle were made by steep lift of the rocks at either side. This was the only good pass across the ridge; it was also the natural watershed for run-off of melted snows, to the eastern and western slopes and valleys. Some jackpine growth dotted the slightly sloping acres and there was a thin seeding of bunch grass and scattering of brush. The two riders, following the clearly marked trail that would take them to the other lip of the pass and so down toward the western slope, came suddenly into view of a handful of buildings lying over near the northern end of the Saddle—a place where the sun could always find them.

Fields were under wire, showing the new green of alfalfa. There was a small flume, obviously built to channel mountain waters to the crops

7

that needed them; constructed crazily of odds and ends, it betrayed its frequent makeshift patchings and repairs. The few buildings, all of them unpainted, took the full beat of the scouring winds that blew here. In the whole place there was no sign that it had known prosperity, yet a great deal of work must have been spent on this little mountain claim.

A look of satisfaction touched the big man's face as he saw it. He said: "Well, there's one bother we're rid of. That's the Harris spread you've heard about. The Saddleback."

The new man surveyed the bleak layout with some interest. "A hell of a place to start a ranch," he muttered.

"All the guy could get," answered Boyden, briefly. "He was nothin' but a damn jail bird—dead broke, couldn't borrow no money, with his record. So he found this place that nobody else wanted, and he's been runnin' his Saddleback iron on some scrub cattle he picked up cheap and spotted in mountain pockets where there's grass part of the year. Put in that alfalfa you see to carry 'em in the feed lots through the winter. And winters are bad up here!"

The smaller man shook his head. "Sounds to me like a tough proposition!"

"Yeah," the other admitted, grudgingly. "I suppose you have to admire the guts behind a thing like that. But he was in the way and had

8

to be got rid of. He won't be bothering us any more."

He stopped suddenly. "Hey, wait a minute, Ivors. Let's drop over that way, since we're here. I just happened to think of something."

It was only a few minutes' ride off the main trail, through straggling bunches of jackpine and juniper. They lost sight of the unpainted buildings, then saw them again and closer. There was a one-room cabin, a shed or two for storing gear and equipment. A rat-tailed nag stood listlessly in the small peeled-pole corral.

Boyden swung down before the cabin, anchoring his mount by the simple procedure of dropping reins into the dust. Without comment, Nate Ivors followed his example. On the ground he fell a good six inches short of the other's solid bulk.

"Only thing this Harris gent had worth owning was a new rifle. Telescopic sights and everything. Guess I might as well pick it up before somebody else beats me to it—if they haven't already!"

"Sure," said the other. "Why not?"

They trailed up the two plank steps and inside the cabin. Like everything else about the place, the furnishings were thrown together from odds and ends, but they were scrupulously neat and clean. There was a puncheon floor, tables and benches made of split logs that showed the marks of the axe-bit. Crude shelves lined the walls,

9

loaded with canned goods and sacks of flour and coffee. One corner was curtained off as a sort of clothes closet. There were carefully made-up bunks against one wall.

But the first thing that caught the eye was the fine bright gleam of the rifle resting on its wall pegs opposite the door. Boyden stepped directly to this and took the piece down; his dark eyes gleamed with admiration as he fondled it, threw the bolt, checked the mechanism of the sights. "A hell of a good weapon!" he grunted, finally hefting it in one thick-fingered hand to feel the balance.

"How do you suppose Harris come by this?"

Ross Boyden shrugged. "Dunno. At any rate, it's a cinch he won't be needing it where he's going!" He cast a glance around the poverty-stricken room. "Nothing else here a white man could use," he grunted. "Let's ride. The boss'll be waiting for us in town."

"Hey!" Nate Ivors exclaimed. "There's some-one outside there."

The big man followed his glance through the tiny window in a side wall of the shack. Some distance up the slope of the Saddle, between the house and the feedlots, a small space had been fenced off for gardening. Unnoticed by them before, a man was at work with a hoe there; the blade of it flashing and dipping in the sun as his back bent to the labour. But even as they watched the man straightened, leaned on the hoe to rest a moment as he ran a shirt sleeve across his forehead. The arm dropped suddenly; the man's glance had lit on the horses standing ground-hitched before the door of the cabin, and an instant attention gripped him.

Big Ross Boyden turned away from the window. "I'd forgot all about that guy," he admitted, carelessly. "A saddlebum Harris picked up somewhere a couple weeks ago to help with the chores—the only kind he could hire."

"What's his name?"

"Damned if I know. Wade something, I think. Forget him!" Boyden had already started for the door. "Come on, let's be going."

The new man tarried for another look out the window. He saw the man in the garden move on a sudden decision; leaving the hoe canted against a fence post, he had slipped through the wire and was coming towards the house at a fast walk. Now as Boyden appeared he switched to a dust-spurting run.

Boyden's saddle boot was empty, and he slipped the rifle into it before he mounted. Ivors came out, leaving the cabin door open, and went to his own bronc. They were like that, reins in hands and about to step up into saddle, when the man came around the side of the building and they heard his crisply spoken: "Hold on here!"

The pair turned slowly, Boyden's heavy face

showing anger, Nate Ivors' only mildly curious. At close range, this man from the garden patch was not very impressive in appearance. He was no more than medium tall, and slight of build. His clothes seemed to hang on him—a tattered shirt, shapeless bib overalls worn outside of scuffed boots. There was no hat on the man's unshorn brown head; his face was a sunburnt red except where a two-day beard stubble covered hollow cheeks. Nate Ivors looked for a holstered gun on the gaunt right thigh, but there wasn't any nor was there a mark where one might ever have been.

His hands were hanging empty at his sides, the fingers opening and closing angrily. Smoky blue eyes ablaze, the man exclaimed: "Just what were the pair of you doing inside the house?"

Scorn touched Boyden's lips, and they barely moved as he said merely: "Don't bother me, bum!"

He turned again to his mount, one hand on the horn to lift himself into saddle. The hand was torn away from there as the man called Wade, taking three quick steps forward, caught him by the shoulder and jerked him around. "I asked you a question!" he snapped, and his voice held an authority strangely belying his appearance. Then his pale eyes caught sight of the rifle in Boyden's saddle boot, and with a start he recognized it. He would have reached and taken it then but the big man knocked his hand away and next minute the man in overalls went sprawling as Boyden's craggy fist smashed full into his face.

He lay in the dust at their feet, a trickle of red beginning at the corner of his mouth, and he stared dazedly as Ross Boyden grunted with studied contempt: "Don't you ever again put your dirty hands on me or my belongings, you damn saddletramp."

Wade passed the back of a hand slowly across his bruised mouth, stared dumbly at the red smear he found on it. Then he raised himself a little from the dust, looking up at Boyden, "That rifle—"

"Now wait!" Boyden cut him off. "Could be you ain't heard. Your boss, Harris, won't need this gun any more. Ain't likely he'll ever be coming back!"

They saw the impact of this news hit the man on the ground, widen his eyes; the smoky-blue of them seemed to darken. He managed: "What-what happened?"

"The law's got him. A stick-up! The man he robbed put a bullet into him—don't know how bad. But even if that don't finish him he'll soon be on his way back to the pen!"

The other got one knee under him, and with a hand pressed against the earth, paused that way as though gathering his strength and letting the effects of that blow he had received clear from his brain. Boyden, his cold-lidded gaze unchanging, went on:

"Lemme just give you some advice. You get a gunnysack and go in the house and fill it up with anything you think you can use. Then sling it behind your kak and drift! Your boss ain't coming home, so there's no reason to stick. And you never know—once the law really starts working on Harris, it might get interested in the saddlebum he's had working for him. I think you see what I mean.

"Me, I don't think I'd wait 'til morning. I'd cinch up and I'd ride—"

That advice given, the big man turned abruptly and nodded at Nate Ivors. "All right! In the saddle!" he ordered. "We've wasted enough time here."

"You're leaving that rifle!"

Ross Boyden quickly whirled, broad face gone livid with anger. The man was on his feet, moving forward. And now Boyden lost his temper.

He met the other with a solid swing of a huge fist. It connected behind the ear, sent the man staggering; but this saddletramp was not to be beaten so easily. Slight as he was compared to Ross Boyden's thick bulk, he came in again and his work-hardened fists, swinging, had a real sting as they landed. Boyden grunted, the blows jarring him. But he stood firm, and then his heavy fists had the drive of pistons as he went after his smaller opponent.

The man would not give ground. Coughing on the dust their boots kicked up, blood smearing the stubble of his lean cheeks, he faced Boyden and fought silently, savagely. Breath gusted as hard fists landed and lungs gave.

Out-matched as he was by the size of Ross Boyden, the slighter man would have been beaten anyway. But the fight was not allowed to run out to a conclusion. Nate Ivors had watched all this with a curious indifference; and now, with the same callous matter-of-factness in his face and manner, he casually drew a long-barrelled six-shooter from his hip holster and stepped in with it ready. Sun winked on blued steel as the gun descended, sharply; he laid it neatly across the back of the smaller man's skull and abruptly the man crumpled, dropped on his face in the dust.

He was still conscious, but there was no fight left in him, or any strength to resist as Ross Boyden swung a boot at his downed opponent. The sharp toe caught the man along the jaw, twisting his head hard about. Ivors stepped in too, then, and for nearly a full minute there was the shuffling of their feet in the milling dust, and the thud of the kicks as they gave this man a working-over with their heavy boots. Ivors lost his hat, blond hair streamed down into his sweating face. Boyden worked methodically, that same furious anger distorting his dark features; and when finally they quit, the big man was panting a little.

Nate Ivors leaned, snagged his hat and beat the dirt out of it and dragged it on, and ran a hairy fist across his jaw to wipe away the sweat. Slowly dust began to settle on the inert and senseless body of the man in the tattered overalls. Ross Boyden spat. "Takes care of *him!*" he muttered; and moving to his horse lifted into saddle.

Ivors followed more slowly, for he was examining his six-shooter to determine that he had not in any way injured its mechanism. There was some dust on the barrel and he took a silk handkerchief from hip pocket and wiped the shining metal clean, lovingly; for Ivors had a craftsman's respect for the tool of his trade.

Then they were both mounted and riding away from that place, without a backward glance. Neither said anything more until they had regained the main trail across the Saddle and it had taken them to the lip of the sharper descent before them.

"Kingdom range just below us," Ross Boyden announced then, shortly. The new man considered the sight. He saw another mountain valley, like the one they had left beyond the Saddle; only larger—almost twice as broad—and it held this difference: water! A river shone yonder like a flash of silver, having its source in the runoff from Old Baldy's icy cap.

Without further words, the two put their horses into the downward trail. They could see, miles ahead, in clear mountain air, the criss-cross of streets and buildings which was the town they aimed for. And Ross Boyden rode with the oiled stock of his stolen rifle thrust forward out of the scabbard, under his thick right knee.

CHAPTER II

It was a long time before the man in the dust made any move, and then the effort forced a groan from his bleeding, battered mouth. He lay after that for some moments, his eyes staring blankly into the white-hot sun, seemingly without thought or feeling. But gradually slow consciousness began to build in him again; it brought blinding waves of pain that surged within his body, and finally it brought a mounting, red tide of fury.

The strength of rage was what got Wade Emery out of the dust, at last. With Ross Boyden's image in his mind, he rolled over, got trembling arms and knees under him and surged to his feet. A half-dozen stumbling strides took him to the door of the cabin; but there he tripped against the two plank steps and fell heavily, his head striking against the jamb of the open door. Panting, he waited for the black mists to swirl away and then, pulling himself up across the sill, lurched on blindly into the cabin. Across the tiny room he spilled his body loosely against the lower of the double bunks; clung to its timbers with one hand while with the other he groped beneath and dragged forth a worn pair of saddlebags. He fumbled with the lashings hastily, prised open the flap and dug within the pockets until his fingers found the cold, hard metal of a six-gun.

The touch of that chill steel seemed to sober him, abruptly. A change came over the man's face, the hot fury that had twisted it giving way to cold calmness. He drew the gun out, looked at it a long moment; but then he shoved it back into the saddlebag and pushed the bag again into the dark opening beneath the bunk.

He dragged himself to his feet, after that, and put both elbows against the upper of the pair of bunks and waited that way until full strength returned. His brain was working clearly now, free of the passion and pain that had blinded him before. He made himself one promise, coldly and dispassionately: he was going to kill Ross Boyden! But with that settled, he could turn his thoughts to the plight of his friend, Joel Harris.

Those thoughts were dark. What was it Boyden had said? Something about an attempt at robbery, and Joel shot? A hard frown carved in his stubble-bearded face, he tried to recall Ross Boyden's exact words. And he had to admit that, on the face of it, the thing was not impossible. His friend had stepped outside the law once before, and served his time for it. Emery supposed he might have done so again.

The battered face of the man was sombre as he considered this. He fumbled absently for the sting of his lower lip, found blood there. Pushing away from the bunk then, he moved unsteadily to a shelf behind the stove and leaned forward to peer at himself in the cracked mirror that was canted against the wall.

Ross Boyden and the other had done their work well. The cut lip was puffed and swelling, and a lump had formed over one eye. The spot at the base of his skull where the six-gun barrel had landed was still numb with pain. It was with some astonishment and great relief that his exploring fingers discovered no ribs caved by the smash of his attackers' heavy boots.

Moving deliberately, he dipped water into a basin and washed his bruised face, carefully. The water in the basin turned red. He used the towel cautiously; considered his features in the glass and thought of a razor with the wistful longing of a man of immaculate habits. He shrugged then, turned to the door, snagging a shapeless hat from a wall peg as he passed. With a hand on the door-latch he paused, considering again the bunk and the six-gun in the saddlebag beneath it. No, he would leave that where it was. Wiser, to go entirely unarmed. He closed the door behind him, clumped down the steps in the full beat of a high sun.

As he went to the shed for his gear, Wade Emery thought of Boyden's advice: *"Get you a gunnysack: fill it with anything you think you can use and drift!"* The memory angered him; and yet in a strange way it was pleasing too—that he had so well-succeeded in the part he had chosen to play. The anonymity of a strictly colourless role had proved, indeed, the best possible shield from curious eyes; eyes that looked without seeing, when a half-way careful glance might have pierced any more elaborate disguise.

But the price was stiff, when a man's pride had to do the paying.

Loaded down with saddle, bridle, and blanket, Emery kicked the tackroom door shut and headed for the small, peeled pole corral. The rat-tailed nag inside the pen rolled its eyes whitely and circled away around the sides as he dropped his gear into the dust and came towards the gate, blunt, scarred hands building a loop in the supple catch-rope. The bronc was an ornery devil; it tried to dodge the cast, but the rope sang out neatly, the loop dropping flat and square across the hammerhead and the string jerking taut as the bronc hit it.

Wade Emery took nothing from the horse. He snubbed it down to one of the corral poles, and let it fight and paw the earth while he went for his gear. Between bucks and pitches he got the blanket on, threw the heavy double-rig saddle into place and caught up the cinches, slipped bridle over the ugly head. Then he leaped to the back of the roan and rode out a brief but sharp flurry of bad acting, before the bronc settled down and trotted out of the corral as sweetly as though that had been all its intention in the first place.

He headed it into the trail that would take him down the western skirt of the Saddle, down to Kingdom Valley and the county seat, through foothill spurs that opened like green and timbered arms with the valley and the shining river stretching away between them. The white-hot sun rode with him, its weight a physical force that bowed his head and shoulders, put the sweat streaming beneath the battered, shapeless hat.

From a distance, the poplars and elms lining the outer streets of the little mountain town suggested shade and coolness; and the park beyond the brief business section, where wild swans swam on the surface of the slowly-flowing river, looked like a pool of green grass and summer comfort. This was an illusion, as the rider quickly learned when his bronc's canter brought him into that deceptive shade. The tree heads seemed to shut the heat in, to concentrate it in stifling folds across sidewalks and rutted roadways. The grass in the park was dry and brittle; and where the sun touched the red roof of the little bandstand by the river bank, it rebounded upwards in shimmering waves that made the eye ache to see them.

Wade Emery rode past the park and up the hill, and entered the district of stores and business buildings. The courthouse filled half a block—an ungainly wooden structure, with its back to the park, and the paint peeling and blistering on the cupola where a few pigeons hovered and moaned and fluttered. Directly across the street, with a few smaller store buildings to separate them, stood the town's two saloons; and as he came abreast of these Emery reined in suddenly, with sudden interest.

The hitchrails before both saloons were crowded with horses—unusual, for the middle of a summer day. The Blue Chip belonged to Thad Kingdom, whose Crown iron dominated all this range west of the mountains; and the broncs racked before its swinging doors all bore Kingdom's familiar four-pronged brand. The horses outside the Clover Leaf also wore a single mark. They were from Steve Mallard's ranch, the Bar M, which lay clear beyond the Saddle and on the dry side of the hill range. To find such a body of Mallard's riders in town was curious; that they should be here on the same day with another size-able group from Crown, was something hinting of real significance.

When he noticed the stolen rifle in the saddle boot of Ross Boyden—Steve Mallard's foreman—quick anger touched Emery. But he turned his back, sent his jughead across the street towards the big courthouse.

On the broad veranda sat Sheriff Dick Rudebaugh with his chair tilted back against the wall. A shotgun leaned nearby, and handy to his big, freckled fist; Rudebaugh liked this weapon and always kept it close to him, a double load of shot in the shining twin barrels. And the solemn look of Rudebaugh's face—the way his blue-eyed gaze never wandered far from the two saloons across the street—showed he knew the potentialities this afternoon held for danger.

Halting in front of the sheriff, Wade Emery leaned with arms folded across the saddlehorn to peer under the edge of the blistered wooden roof. "Kind of warm," he suggested.

Out of the shadows the other gave him the briefest of looks. As some men can read an entire page of a book with one flick of an eye, so the sheriff could read a man completely in the same way; it was a spare economy of attention his job had taught him. This put an uneasiness in Emery but Dick Rudebaugh had swung his keen gaze from him and was again towards the scene across the street. His was a great, shaggy head, leonine of profile, and burnt as dark as the leather of his boots. He reached into a pocket of an unbuttoned vest, dragged out a huge turnip watch; flicked it briefly with his glance and stuffed it back into its pocket.

"Expecting someone?"

The sheriff shrugged, spoke in a voice that was a deep bass rumble. "Just expecting all the trouble on this range to come roost in my office ten minutes from now, is all. You know why? It's because, like a damn fool, I went and sent out a call inviting Steve Mallard and old man Kingdom to get together with me this afternoon and see if we can't find a way to thrash out this water situation. Yeah, I did that!"

Emery said: "Well, looks like they came."

"And brought their armies with them! Hell of a way to make a peace talk, ain't it? At three o'clock the fireworks is gonna start—if it don't start sooner!" He turned on the other fully, then. "So you better ride someplace else, mister. You're obstructin' my view!"

Emery straightened. "Sheriff, I was wanting to speak to—"

"Your boss is down at the Franz house," Rudebaugh cut in impatiently. "Doc Franz wanted him taken there instead of put in a cell, the bullet hole in him being the shape it is; says the guy needs some work done on him. You'll find him there."

Emery gave a short nod. "Thanks." Riding on along the street, he guessed that Rudebaugh's troubles were too big and too many for him to give more than half a thought to anyone as insignificant as Joel Harris or the drifter who worked for him. And that was all to the good!

The doctor's small house, a block or two off Main Street, sat circled by a sagging fence that needed painting. The drooping flowers about the porch were not dead as they looked, because this western slope was overdue for a rain and when it came they would pick up miraculously—that was the way of the country. The gate lacked a hinge, so that it dragged the ground and had to be lifted and moved aside carefully. Emery walked up the dusty path and the short step to the porch, and put his raw, work-tough knuckles against the door. Curtains at the window stirred; then there were quick steps and a girl opened to him.

She should have been a pretty girl, but life had not been kind to her. She was too thin. Work had fined her down and reddened and roughened her strong, capable hands, and some too constant worry had put a shadow into her blue eyes. The corn-yellow hair that might have softened the sharp contours of her face had no chance to do so, for she wore it tied up with an old cotton handkerchief that was faded but clean. The house dress she wore was the kind that a person could do a lot of work in without its showing the dirt, or wearing out.

Wade Emery said: "The sheriff told me Joel Harris is in this house."

The hand on the edge of the door tightened, and the thin face tightened too, around the mouth. "Who are you?" she demanded. "What do you want?" She was staring at him, and not liking what she saw.

He felt ill at ease. He ran a knuckle across the lower edge of his jaw, heard the rasp of the beard stubble against it. When he tried to smile, reassuringly, the split lip stretched and stung. He said: "I just wanted to see him, miss. For a few seconds. I'm Wade Emery—I work for Harris. Perhaps he mentioned—"

"Oh." A different light came behind her eyes. "Of course." She stepped back, making room for him, and he came through the door dragging off the shapeless hat. "I was just a little uneasy at first. Father isn't—isn't here. But you're a friend of Joel's. Of course."

"Thanks." He added: "I guess I don't look too good to go calling. I wouldn't blame you for not letting me in."

A faint colour touched her cheeks. "Please—" She gestured quickly to a door that opened, half ajar, off the neat but poorly-furnished sitting-room. "He's in there."

Wade nodded and went past her. As he did so he noticed, on the round centre table, a shabby beaver hat and a black doctor's bag whose leather looked split at the folds, its clasp tarnished. There was something else on the table beside the bag; the girl, seeing the direction of his glance, moved in quickly and put herself before the table in a too-casual attempt to shield it from him. But Emery had seen, and it told him a great deal about this house and its problems. For the object was an empty whisky bottle.

CHAPTER III

"Wade!" Alarm was in Joel Harris's voice. "Good lord! You shouldn't have come—"

Emery asked quietly: "How bad are you hurt, Joel?"

The other flicked a glance down the long length of his body, underneath the sheet. "Only my knee. But it was smashed up some—Doc says I'll probably always limp." There was bitterness in the words.

His bed stood near the window, where a drawn shade let in any breeze but none of the glare. A pair of childish voices shouted in the yard. The young woman said from the doorway: "Have those kids been keeping you awake, Joel? I ought to have shut them up!"

"It's all right, Terry." He added: "I'd like to sit up for a little. It gets monotonous in one position."

Wade helped him ease up to a half-sitting position, and arranged the pillow at his back. The sheet was hot to the touch. He noticed how gently and tenderly Terry Franz administered to her patient. Something about this made him ask, when she had left the room: "You've known the girl long, Joel?"

"Terry Franz? Nearly a year, I suppose."

"Seems very nice."

Joel nodded absently. "Sure. Poor kid has a tough time, with Chris and Jim to look after and a no-good father that drinks up every fee he manages to collect." But his thoughts were not really on her and he said again, abruptly: "Why did you come? You should stay away from this town!"

Wade Emery dragged a chair over and let himself upon the edge of it, dropped his dusty hat to the floor beside runover boots. "I had to talk to you, Joel." Suddenly the other was sitting forward, dark glance widening.

"Have you been fighting?" He was seeing now, for the first time, the battered condition of Wade's features. "Looks like a hell of a scrap—"

His friend shrugged. "Talk about that some other time. I want the straight on the news that came up to me, at the spread."

"The fight came with the news, I guess," Joel Harris suggested shrewdly. A sour look settled over his dark, handsome face. He was a year or so younger than Emery, but the time he had spent in prison must have been what put the lines about his eyes and mouth and made him look older than he was. Prison, too, had stamped the whole cast of his face with a bitterness time had not smoothed out, because the bitterness was stamped into his mind, as well.

Scowling at the bedclothes now, he muttered:

30

"You know what I am, I guess—what I do when I get desperate and in bad need of cash. Maybe you thought I was cured after that term in stony lonesome; but you know different now! So use your brains and ride out of this set-up before you get yourself into trouble for no damn good reason!"

Wade Emery was silent for some time, his pale blue eyes studying the face of the other that was turned half away from him, not meeting his glance. "I could be a fool," he admitted then, without rancour, "but I'm not so stupid I can't tell when you're lying. So quit trying it—and tell me exactly what you're supposed to have done, and how it happened!"

"All right!" The hurt man's jaw was tight, the skin stretching pale across the cheek muscles underneath. "Somebody stuck up Thad Kingdom this morning, on the way out to his ranch with the monthly payroll. Or at least so Thad says. The man was masked, of course, but somehow I was recognized."

"And where were you really at the time?"

"Riding up to Saddleback! I came down today, you know, to talk to Phil Nolan at the store and see if he'd carry me on the books a little longer. He said no! That put me in a pretty sour mood, and I'm afraid I talked some about how bad I needed money. Maybe Kingdom heard, and that helped him identify me later. Or maybe—"

"Maybe he lied? Would he have had any reason to do that?"

The sharpening of Joel's face told that there was such a reason, but for a long time he would not speak what was on his mind. But Emery waited, and at last he dragged it out and made a face over the words: "There's Lynne! Reason enough, I suppose. Kingdom has no heart—he's utterly cold and ruthless. This is just the sort of thing he would do to break up his daughter's friendship with an ex-convict!" Joel shrugged, heavily. "Anyway, he sent his men out to get me, and they picked me up at the foot of the Saddle. There was shooting—Bart Yaeger, I think, started it—and they brought me to town. Like this!"

There was silence for some moments. Through it they heard Terry Franz at the side door calling to her brother and sister, and the noisy trooping of the children into the house. Wade Emery said, slowly:

"And you wanted to make me think you were guilty—to think you'd sidestepped again, the way you did three years ago—so I'd ride away and save my own hide! You couldn't have made it stick, Joel."

"Maybe not," Joel grunted. "But it was worth a try. It's too great a risk for you to mix into this thing. You'd attract too much attention. First thing you knew Dick Rudebaugh would notice your face and it would jog his memory, and he'd start going through his reward dodgers. And there's not much hope for me, you know—my word against Thad Kingdom's!"

"That remains to be seen," said Emery. "Few frame-ups are perfect. There may be a way to crack this one."

He stood up, snagging his battered Stetson from the floor. Joel Harris exclaimed: "What do you intend to do?"

"I don't say that I know. But you're as well off lying there as any place while that leg knits up. And I'll be moving around, keeping my eyes open." He added: "You didn't hesitate to take me in and hide me from the law when I needed it. Maybe I haven't forgotten, even if you have!" He put a hand on the hurt man's shoulder, then; just a touch of the fingers, and just a touch of a smile crossing his bruised lips as he said: "Well, take it easy!"

He went quickly from the bedroom, out into the front of the little house. He noticed that Terry Franz had quietly removed the tell-tale bottle from beside her father's hat and bag. He supposed there was some other bedroom where Doc Franz was now hard at work sleeping off a whisky jag.

At the front door he turned, glimpsed the kitchen past a cheap muslin curtain, and a boy and girl of eight or ten eating bread and butter there, and drinking milk their sister had poured for them out of a large, cracked pitcher. Terry Franz rose from the kitchen table and came out to him, the children watching wide-eyed across their mugs of foaming white milk.

"Thank you," he said, "for letting me see him." He added, hesitating: "If you heard anything of what we said, I—trust you won't repeat it."

"Oh, no!" she exclaimed, on a breathless tone, her blue eyes wide in the thin, pale face. "And I wasn't eavesdropping!"

"I didn't mean that," he assured her, quickly. He would have said more but the voice of Joel Harris, calling from the bedroom, cut him off.

"Wade!" And when Emery answered: "One thing I wish you could find out for me."

"Yes, Joel?"

"Try and learn what Lynne Kingdom has heard, and what she thinks!"

"Of course," said Wade Emery. And he saw the Franz girl's glance waver, pain flick across her face. Feeling his eyes on her, she managed somehow to summon up a smile for him, and she said "Good afternoon" almost as though Joel's words had not taken a bad wrench at her heart.

He had some wry thoughts as he went back down the path, closed the broken gate carefully, and swung up into the frayed, patched saddle. They were three of a kind really—Wade and Joel and this girl. Three to whom fate had dealt some rather messy hands. Joel, forever branded with a bad name because of a youthful mis-step for which he had paid the full penalty in prison horror, and now due to be railroaded back to the pen just when the hill ranch on which he'd laboured was beginning to produce, to pay off Wade himself, hounded across the land for a killing which had been done in self-defence but which the law and his enemies chose to call murder. And now, Terry Franz with her overload of toil and the shame of a drunken father—and the hopeless love to which Joel Harris was blinded by his own feelings for the wealthy, beautiful Lynne Kingdom. . . .

It was all very strange, and troubling . . . Wade Emery dismissed these thoughts when, turning into Main Street, he passed a watchmaker's shop on the corner and heard a big clock inside the low, shadowy building strike the hour, solemnly, the beats pulsing out slow and heavy upon the breathless air. In the window of the shop, the hands of a dozen display watches all pointed, carefully, at three. He remembered, then, what Dick Rudebaugh had said was due to happen at this hour.

He walked his jughead slowly along the dusty strip, and some twenty yards from the courthouse reined in and sat forward a little in the saddle, watching. Already armed men were coming out of the two big saloons across the street from the sheriff's office, and trailing in two tight groups to converge on the wooden steps of the sprawling courthouse veranda. He saw tall, white-haired Thad Kingdom, lean as a rail and boot-tough. He thought one of the three men with him must be his Crown iron foreman, Chuck Short, although Wade did not know Short by sight. He recognized Bart Yaeger, however, and a chill crept into Emery's glance as it lay on the hump-shouldered figure of the man who had shot Joel Harris.

As the group from Crown reached the steps they met the other party that was coming in answer to Dick Rudebaugh's summons. Ross Boyden and Nate Ivors were there, and their boss. Wade switched his glance, looked with interest on this Steve Mallard whose spread, the Bar M, lay on the dry slope beyond the Saddle and who was a threat to the peace, the established order of things, here on Kingdom range.

He saw a stocky man of medium height, powerfully-built, with rather heavy brows that seemed to lie as a weight across his eyes and drag them into a perpetual scowl. His nose was a little crooked, his mouth full and sullen. He was dressed carelessly, in hardworn riding clothes and a black, broad-brimmed Stetson, and he strode at the head of his men with a firm pace that kicked the dust high in front of him. When he reached the foot of the courthouse steps at the same moment as old Thad Kingdom, the pair of them hauled up and looked at each other, neither giving way, a challenge passing wordlessly between them.

Dick Rudebaugh had come out of the shadows and he waited at the top of the steps, the sun putting its hard glare across the lower part of his body and glinting from the shining twin muzzles of the shotgun the sheriff held, loosely cradled. Perhaps to the men below him, the sight of that gun was a suggestion, a caution.

At any rate, Steve Mallard, who had seemed on the verge of elbowing Thad Kingdom to one side, now stepped back leaving a space clear for the older man and he said, with mocking humour in his voice: "After you, sir!" Old Kingdom gave him a look that was veiled by blue-veined lids, and then he went up the steps, straight as a ramrod, his men following in a ragged thunder of boots on the dry boards. Rudebaugh stepped aside for them, motioning towards the gaping door of the building with a nod of his shaggy head. The Crown owner had one boot lifted to the sill when a remark from Ross Boyden, below in the dust, caused him to halt and turn.

Boyden had caught sight of Wade Emery, watching this scene from horseback not many yards away. A humourless grin tilted the corners of the Bar M ramrod's flat-lipped mouth, as he sang out: "Oh—so you're drifting, huh? Decided to take my suggestion?"

Wade Emery straightened quickly as Boyden's

words struck him. He had not wanted to be brought into this, nor did he like having the attention of all those men suddenly centred on him. He saw Thad Kingdom staring with sharp brown eyes, felt the keen gaze of Steve Mallard's narrow, black ones. And across the wide street, he could see the shine of sunlight on the stock of Joel Harris's stolen rifle, thrusting up from the boot of Boyden's saddle, and that reminder of the score he had to settle with Ross Boyden did nothing to help him with the humble role he had to play.

He put out the edge of his tongue, wet dust-dry lips. He muttered: "I—thought over some what you said."

"That's being smart!" grunted the Bar M foreman. And then indifferently he turned his back.

But Thad Kingdom had left the courthouse entrance and he came to the railing now, put his hands on it and leaned forward sharply. "You!" he barked at Emery, and the man in the saddle reined around to face him. Kingdom was only a little above him. He could see the cords standing out on the old man's neck, that was rough and raw-looking like the jowls of a turkey. "Are you that saddletramp who worked for Harris?"

Emery hesitated, then nodded. "Yes. That's me, I guess."

"Sheriff!" snorted old Kingdom, then. "I want you to arrest this man and hold him for questioning! Remember, you haven't found the money his boss stole from me this morning, and I don't think we ought to let this fellow drift until you do. It might be in his saddle-pocket, for all we know. Or he may savvy where it's hidden."

The sheriff's brow dragged down, and he ran the broad thumb of one hand up and down the front of his vest a moment, while he pondered seemingly in doubt. He said finally, in his deep rumble of a voice: "Oh, I dunno, Thad. He wasn't anywhere around at the time of the stick-up, was he? And we figure Harris must have managed to get rid of the money before we caught up with him—if it was him did it, of course."

"Why do you say 'if'?" demanded Kingdom, turning on the officer. "He was recognized!"

Rudebaugh shrugged a little. "All right—all right. But anyway, I got my doubts that this gent here was in on the job."

"You want to search me, Sheriff?" asked Wade Emery suddenly.

"Naw!" Rudebaugh seemed suddenly impatient with the whole procedure. He flapped a broad hand at Wade negatively, and then he was between Thad Kingdom and the rail and he was herding the old rancher towards the door. "We got business inside, gents!" he grunted. "Time's awearin'."

Thad Kingdom did not want to be budged. "Now, you listen, Sheriff—" he began, on a rising tone. He stopped speaking suddenly, his expression changing, faded brown eyes on the sheriff as though he were listening to something the other was saying, for his ears only. Then his whole manner altered abruptly and with a nod Kingdom turned, no longer arguing, and preceded the sheriff in through the door of the courthouse.

Bart Yaeger and the other Crown men followed, and then Steve Mallard went clumping up the steps and, with his followers trailing, he also disappeared into the shadow of the building. Silence settled upon the street, then, and Wade Emery was alone.

Voices were coming faintly now through the open window of the sheriff's office; he could see the faint shapes of men settling down in there for the meeting Dick Rudebaugh had called. Wade straightened in the saddle, laid a look around him. Men were watching in doors and windows of neighbouring buildings. He knew they had witnessed the whole scene, and that their unfriendly eyes were on him.

He shook out the reins then and he touched a spurless heel to his mount's flank and left that place. The things he had seen and heard were a jumble within his mind, as he rode out past the drooping trees of the park, and the red-roofed bandstand that sent back the sun's rays in a bright, shimmering smear, downslope beside the river. He took the trail to the Saddle, letting the bronc hit a rolling stride that ate up the miles. He rode straight in saddle, a gaunt and shabby figure with uncertainty and suspicion printed in his red-burnt, stubble-bearded face.

CHAPTER IV

Before going in to the meeting Dick Rudebaugh nodded to his deputy, Lee Ball, who had been waiting in the hall to be on hand if his boss needed him. "Come here, Lee." He drew him aside, spoke swiftly, his deep voice a mere rumble in the dark hallway. "I want you to saddle and follow that drifter. If he heads west, out of the valley, let him go. But if he starts up towards the Saddle keep on his tail and try not to let him see you."

The deputy looked puzzled. "What's the deal?"

"He's just been down to the doc's—probably talking things over with Harris. If Harris actually pulled that hold-up this morning, then it's got to be that he buried the money someplace between where it happened, and where Kingdom's men picked him up. If so, chances are he's told this drifter where to look and the man will ride to get it. Of course, on the other hand he might not trust Emery, thinking the gent would pocket the cash and hit the trail for good. Depends on how much Harris trusts him."

Ball said, "I see. So if this tramp heads for the money, what do I do?"

"Wait till he gets his hands on it, then pick him up and bring him in."

"And if he don't?"

"Then let him go and come on back to town and report to me. That's all, Lee."

He started to turn away, but the deputy looked uncertain. "What about this thing here, chief? Won't you be needing me?"

Rudebaugh shrugged wide shoulders, his leonine face impassive. "Nothing's happened yet but talk. Maybe I can keep it on that basis. No, I want you on Emery's trail; I had to promise old man Kingdom I'd send you, before he'd shut up and calm down at all."

"All right—just as you say, chief." Lee rung his spurs down the long hall, and Dick Rudebaugh turned to his office where he found the men from Crown and from Bar M waiting, in heavy silence, for him to start the meeting he had had the temerity to summon.

He felt the tension that strung between the two groups of men, and knew that the whole weight and responsibility lay squarely on him. None of these would make any move to ease the burden of it, and that thought angered him. But he let none of this show on his broad, square face. He started to shut the door, changed his mind. "Better have what breeze we can get through here," he muttered.

Eight men in this little room filled it to overflowing. There were only chairs for three. Steve Mallard had taken one by the window, and he teetered there on its stiff legs, looking at his ease with thumbs shoved into armholes of his vest. Thad Kingdom sat stiff and straight on the edge of another chair in one corner, his expensive flat-crowned white hat held carefully on his bony knees. They had left the sheriff's swivel chair by the desk empty, and he clumped over and settled there, whirling it around to face the room and with big hands spread upon his thighs. The shotgun leaned against a corner of the desk, close to his hand as usual. The horsey, sweaty smell of outdoor men was heavy in the close warm air.

Rudebaugh scowled at the rest of the men ranged, stiff and uneasy, along the wall. "You gents make me uncomfortable, standing up like that," he growled. "The floor's nice and soft. I wan't figuring on such a crowd or I'd have hired the Odd Fellows' Hall; but since you're here you can at least squat down on your spurs and make yourselves at home."

Ross Boyden cleared his throat, shot a quick look at his boss. "I'd rather stand," he muttered. Like every other man in the room, he had his gun strapped on and in that position it hung close and handy below the strike of blunt fingers.

The sheriff ran a slow glance around the circle of men—at Boyden, and Nate Ivors whom he didn't know; at Bart Yaeger and foreman Chuck Short and the other Crown men. Then he gave a sigh and swivelling his chair to face Steve

Mallard directly, blurted out bluntly: "What are you going to do about that water, Steve?"

Mallard let his chair legs down quickly, anger showing in his sullen face. "Did you bring me here, all the way across the Saddle, just to ask me that? You already know what I'm going to do—I've made no secret about it! I'm going to dynamite that slide and get my water flowing again!"

"Just try it!" said Chuck Short, across the room. "You'll start hot lead flowing when you do!" The Crown foreman was a heavy-lidded, lantern-jawed man of forty whose floppy Stetson, sewn around the brim with rawhide, was pushed back enough to show tawny hair that was getting sparse in front. He barely parted his lips when he spoke, let the words slide out thinly.

Ross Boyden growled: "Shut your trap, Short, or I'll lay nine inches of blue gun-barrel across it!"

"All right now!" growled Dick Rudebaugh, and before his tone the thread of violent talk snapped and the room went silent again. But he was beginning to doubt that he could control this thing that he had started. He went ahead with it, doggedly.

"You know of course, Steve, why the folks on this side are so plumb set against you trying a thing like what you plan? They figure it's not their fault that rock slide happened, up there in the hills, and blocked the springs you'd been using. They don't think they should have to take the risk of having the water sources here on the west side of the Saddle disrupted."

"There's no risk to it!" Mallard retorted, promptly. "I've had a geologist up there to look the thing over and report on the possibilities. I'm convinced the job can be done easily, and without any danger to anyone."

"*I'm* not convinced!" cried Thad Kingdom. His head was shot forward on its turkey-gobbler neck, brown eyes flashing fire. "It would take a hell of a lot of dynamite to move that slide. I'll not have you monkeying with it!"

Steve Mallard got quiet. But his hands were clenched on his knees, and the heavy black brows weighed down upon his eyes with a scowl that gave Dick Rudebaugh a creepy feeling. He felt himself caught in the middle between these two men, who sat in opposite corners of the room; that they had taken the reins out of his hands and were running this thing now on a sure road to violence.

Mallard said: "Have any of you been across the Saddle lately, to see how it is with that east slope range? It's shot to hell! Here on the west you at least get the rains—I don't even have that. Another season like this and the grass will be gone—and when it goes it won't come back; you know that! D'you expect me to sit and watch my ranch and my graze burn up and do nothing about it—when there's even the slightest chance that I can unstop that slide with a few sticks rightly placed, and start the streams and springs flowing again?"

"Yeah, I've seen your graze, Mallard!" answered Thad Kingdom, flatly. "And all I know is I'm not gonna have the same thing happen to Kingdom Valley! I'll back what I say with guns, too. This is warning: You keep away from that slide—keep clear out of that up-country!"

Steve Mallard came to his feet, with a gracefulness surprising in one of so stocky a build. He said, crisply: "That sounds like an ultimatum, Thad Kingdom!"

"It is!" answered Kingdom, rising too. He was the tallest man in the room—a long, gaunt beanpole of toughness. "Stay on your side of the Saddle. Stay out of Kingdom. And don't let me catch one whiff of dynamite—or it'll be showdown between the east slope and the west!"

The man from east of the Saddle turned to Dick Rudebaugh then, and spread his hands a little. "There it is, Sheriff. Nothing much more to say, do you think?"

Rudebaugh, the only man seated now, canted his head up at them and the broad features of the sheriff were stony with disappointment. "No," he admitted, nodding heavily. "I guess there's not. I guess there's nothing for me to do now but give you this!"

He turned, fished into the welter of papers that littered his desk and crammed the dusty pigeonholes, and with unerring sureness found the document he wanted. Without glancing at it he handed the paper to Steve Mallard.

The other's scowl deepened with suspicion. He took the paper, distrustfully. He said, curtly: "What the hell is this?"

"An injunction," muttered the sheriff, not looking at him squarely. "Issued by Judge Clayborn when he was here last week, at the request of Thad Kingdom as representative of the ranchers of the west slope. It forbids you to tamper with that slide."

"Oh."

Fury darkened the black eyes; the mouth under the twisted nose made a grimace of rage. "Forbids me, eh?" The paper in Mallard's hand crumpled under the squeeze of white-knuckled fingers. "I'll take this damn piece of paper and I'll—"

"Careful!" the sheriff cautioned him, sharply. "It ain't quite the same proposition, now. I wanted to be able to keep out of this," he went on, throwing a dark look at old Kingdom. "I think I see both sides of the problem, and I savvy what you both stand to gain and lose. But—" He shrugged, pushed up from the swivel chair to face the roomful of men. "When an injunction's served, I have to enforce it. And I'll do just that! So just keep it in mind, Steve Mallard, before you tear up that paper!"

Triumph made old Thad Kingdom's face an unpleasant thing to see, then, and the black fury struggling behind the Bar M rancher's eyes was no better to look at. If there was to be a break, Dick Rudebaugh thought, it would come now; and Mallard would start it. Because Kingdom had already gained what he wanted, with the serving of that injunction. It was now Steve Mallard's move, and any violence on his part would mean a clear breaking of the law.

But the law, after all, was only one man, and that man was Dick Rudebaugh. He was suddenly utterly sick of the whole confused mess, and unspeakably angry with Thad Kingdom for having—brutally, callously—thrown the whole weight of the thing upon his shoulders with this move.

Then he breathed easier as he saw, by Steve Mallard's eyes, that this was not to be the time. The Bar M rancher backed down. He did it in a way that was purely typical. He merely jerked his head at his foreman; growled, "Ross!" and turning, shouldered past the sheriff and strode out of the office.

Ross Boyden looked as though he would have liked to burn a little powder, but he did not hesitate. Chuck Short and Yaeger were grinning, openly, and the smug satisfaction on old Kingdom's harsh, seamed face looked like a snarl of triumph. Ross ignored them all and, face expressionless, strode after his boss. Without asking, Nate Ivors made up the tail.

At the door, however, Nate turned for a slow look at the Crown men, and at Dick Rudebaugh. The new Bar M gunhand looked as though he had been enjoying a show, and wanted a last pleased glance at the actors who had entertained him. Then he jerked on his Stetson with lean, freckled hand, and turning his back rang his spurs, nonchalantly and unhurriedly, out of the office.

He heard, behind him, the sheriff's grunt: "Well, I hope you're satisfied all to hell, Thad!" And old Kingdom's gloating: "Why shouldn't I be? I got what I wanted . . ."

A thoroughly unscrupulous character, Nate Ivors thought—a man to tickle the sandy-haired gunman's fancy. He wouldn't have minded packing his iron on the other side in this quarrel, now that he'd seen the kind of ranny old Kingdom was, but he didn't let it bother him. Cash on the barrelhead was the basis on which Nate hired out his gun and the speed of his arm.

Boyden and Steve Mallard were across the street, lifting into saddle, as he came down the sun-warped steps and the hand of the sun hit him again. Nate Ivors found his own mount in the line at the hitchrack and checked the cinches, was stepping up as Mallard's voice rapped out against the silence of the street. "Bar M! Outside!"

Now other riders were filing out of the Clover Leaf, the batwings busy as they came shoving through and without instructions sought their horses. There were a half-dozen of them—the bulk of Steve Mallard's crew, that he had brought with him and kept in reserve against a possible need for them, if the meeting in the sheriff's office had gone badly. Their passage built thunder and a screen of blowing dust along the street as one by one they found stirrups and strung out after their chief, who had already taken the trail with Ross Boyden siding him and Ivors close behind. They were a hard and dangerous sight—enough to leave warning in the air behind them as the cavalcade filed out of town. Crown men pushed open the door of the Blue Chip, stood bunched watching them go in utter silence. Across the street, on the veranda of the courthouse, Thad Kingdom and his foreman stood, also watching. And at the window of his office, Dick Rudebaugh's face showed, grim and troubled.

As the town fell away and the lift of the Saddle showed ahead, across rolling range of bluestem, Ross Boyden kneed in close to his boss and above the rhythmic pound of hoofbeats asked him: "What do you think?"

Steve Mallard turned on him a face that was broken in a crooked smile of satisfaction. "That damn fool Kingdom!" he muttered, eyes showing pleasure under the level ridge of heavy brows. "He's rising to the bait even better than I could have hoped. He's playing right into our hands!"

"What are you going to do about that injunction?"

For answer, Mallard reached into his pocket and drew the paper forth. He looked at it a moment, and then calmly tore the document into a dozen pieces and held them up on open palm, to let the wind pick them from his hand and send them fluttering away behind him in a stream. He looked at Boyden then, sidelong, the heavy brow lifted at one corner. "We'll go ahead as we planned. Step by step."

"The Harris place?" suggested his foreman, his eyes on the Saddle scooping into the white-capped skyline ahead under the blazing blue of the sky.

"I'll leave that in your hands. Take some of the boys and move in tonight if you feel like."

Boyden nodded. "Tonight," he repeated. "Sure— why not?"

After that they rode in silence, the cavalcade of men strung out behind them along the tawny road, dust funnelling high under loping hoofs.

53

Sun touched and glinted from harness trappings, from holstered guns and filled cartridge belts, and the gleam of rifle metal in the saddle boots.

CHAPTER V

Thought of the man who had trailed him out of town was an irritant to Wade Emery, that plagued him continually as the long evening wore on. He did not know Lee Ball by sight, and the deputy kept too great a distance for Wade to see him plainly or the markings on his horse; but not knowing only added to his uneasiness. He had a feeling that Dick Rudebaugh had sent the rider, and he could only wonder why. He asked himself with misgivings if the sheriff could be growing suspicious.

There was no answer to these questions, and they stayed as a pricking in his mind while he finished the chores around the spread, and fried up a mess of eggs and ham and brewed coffee on the small woodstove. Night was only a smoky haze across that high country, as he finished his meal and cleaned up the dishes. Emery went to the door of the shack, looked out across the thinly-timbered sweep of the Saddle to where it broke against the jagged rocks of the yonder wall. Shadows were gathering in the juniper clumps and the hollows of the pass, while the white peak of Baldy reared up pink and gold in the last rays of the vanished sun. A star burned, bright and sharp, alone in the deepening sky. A wind was washing down from the upward snowfields, with the coming of darkness; it warped the air with its chill.

He could not see the trail from this door but he had heard, hours before, the echo of hoofbeats that rocketed back from the bleak walls and told of a large number of horsemen heading east through the gap. Bar M, he thought, and wondered about the sheriff's meeting. And that put him in mind of Ross Boyden's earlier visit, and he drew from that a half-felt warning that he decided best not to ignore.

A rifle stood in the corner by the bunks, with a new box of shells on a shelf above it. He took these suddenly, and from the clothes closet behind the curtained partition, he got a heavy sheep-lined jacket that belonged to Joel Harris. Coming out, leaving the house dark and the door standing open, Wade hurried to the corral where the jugheaded roan was penned.

There was a rope hackamore on the bronc's head. Without bothering for a saddle, he opened the gate and went in to the fidgety animal and got a hold of the rope, and balancing the rifle in his other hand led it away from there. He took the roan a quarter of a mile to a hidden graze he knew about, and left it there without hobbles because he was sure the roan would not stray from good grass. Full dark had descended by the time he returned to the ranch, afoot, and with it a feeling of tense expectancy gripped him.

Just behind the buildings and the corral and the wired garden patch rose the back of the Saddle, steeply—a face of barren and eroded rock. There was a straggle of vegetation among the talus slanting up to the foot of the wall. Wade Emery went into this, found himself a spot behind a stunted windfall cedar and settled down there to wait, laying the rifle across the trunk and hunkering behind it.

He was glad now for the sheepskin. He dragged it closer about his throat, tucked thinly-clad legs beneath him as the chill of the rocks and the night breeze came into his body. Below, under increasing starlight, Saddleback Ranch looked utterly deserted and ghostly, the door of the shack opening blackly on a dark interior, the corral empty. A hoot-owl sounded off somewhere down in the shallow bowl of the pass; a bat skimmed across the sky on silent wings. Wade could hear the gurgle of water in the flumes, see the faint shimmer of starlight on distant snowfields, catch the sweet and tangy scent of sage and cedar.

Time dragged out; he began to wonder if his hunch was a poor one. Then the sound of horses came up to him, unmistakably, and silently Wade Emery raised for a look. Presently he was rewarded by the sight of a group of horsemen coming at a walk from the straggle of timber over towards the trail, and into the clearer stretch that led up to the ranch itself.

There was no moon, but he could see the figures blackly. Four riders. As they came nearer he eased down, prone, and he brought the rifle to him and cuddled his cheek to the stock. It was cold against his face. He lined up a tentative bead on the bare space before the dark door of the house, and waited that way for the right moment. . . .

Boyden had brought Nate Ivors with him, and Jeff Bushong and Charlie Rook. They drew into a knot and halted their horses for a careful inspection of the silent ranch, and Ross Boyden said, presently: "See, the door's standing open. No bronc in the pen. The guy's gone, all right."

"Looks that way," said Ivors. "Can't always tell by looks, though."

The foreman frowned in the darkness. He didn't like being contradicted, and yet he knew Ivors had a lot of right on his side and that made it even less pleasant. The new Bar M gunhand, he realized, was an extremely careful man; it was that very caution which made Nate Ivors dangerous.

Stubbornly, the leader said: "He's gone, I tell you—he was on his way out when we saw him down below. Nothing to do here but walk in!" And he touched spurs to his bay's flanks and moved forward. There was no more argument, whatever Nate Ivors or the rest might be thinking, and they were close behind Boyden as he walked his horse up the slight rise and, not far from the house, lit down. They did likewise, leaving the broncs on trailing reins.

Utter silence held, except for the rattle of scrub brush in the night breeze and other small, normal sounds. Suddenly Ross Boyden didn't like this proposition, but he had made his brag and frowning he thought: What am I afraid of—that saddletramp? He said gruffly: "Come on!"

He was only yards from the door when a rifle slug whined thinly past and clapped smartly into the face of the building.

Instinctively he ducked, heard behind him Jeff Bushong's startled yell. Ross Boyden did not even know where that shot had come from, but another followed it, and another. They were much too close. He hit the dirt, rolling; got his feet under him again and was up scampering back to join the other three.

"He's up at the base of the rocks," announced Nate Ivors, calmly. "I saw the flashes. Good shooting, if he meant to scare you; because it sure looks like that's what he did!"

"Shut up!"

The Bar M foreman was raging inwardly at the ludicrous figure he must have made scrambling away from the rifle fire. "That damned tramp!"

he growled. He too had seen the flashes and knew roughly where the sniper was hidden. "Get your rifles! We'll clean him out!"

He felt more confident when the weapon he had stolen that morning was in his hands. He was thinking better now. "Ivors!" he ordered. "You and Jeff Bushong swing out and circle up past where he's holed in. Charlie and I will keep him busy from here. We'll smear him all over the face of that cliff!"

Nate Ivors looked at him, seeing him only dimly in the starlight, and then he looked over at the dark lift of rocks where the enemy was hidden. The new man frowned, opened his mouth to give protest; but Boyden had already turned away and Bushong was starting off in the direction the foreman indicated. Ivors clamped his jaw on unspoken words, gave a shrug of indifference. He started after Bushong at a slow jog.

Boyden was a fool, he thought, to believe that man on the hill was going to let himself be trapped by so simple a manoeuvre. He had a lot of new respect, himself, for this drifter they were up against. Ivors had been around enough to know good shooting when he saw it, and the man who had handled that rifle was a master. Only an expert could have put his shots so exactly at such distance, and working only by starlight! It would never do to underestimate Wade Emery.

Well, it was none of his business; all he had to lose was his own skin, and first, last and always it was Nate Ivors' prime concern to keep that skin whole and in one piece. Being forewarned, he thought he should come out of this set-up intact.

Bushong was ahead of him, jogging against the stars, and Ivors followed at an easy pace with rifle held at the balance. They had rounded the corral, and now wire gleamed faintly and clods of soft earth crumbled underfoot as they made their way along the side of the fenced-off garden plot. Then there were rocks, and weeds, and rougher going as the ground began to lift suddenly. Down yonder, Ross Boyden and Charlie Rook had opened up with their rifles, their song a thin, high snapping on the night wind. It was random firing, supposed to cover this flanking movement. Nate Ivors didn't think the lone man was fooled. He had an uneasy feeling Emery could see him and Bushong coming plainly.

He got confirmation of this when the rifle in the rocks sounded, from a new position. Nate Ivors dropped, hugging the ground. And at the same moment there was a shrill scream ahead of him and Bushong went down, brush crackling as his body flopped into it.

Damned fool! thought Ivors. Skylining himself—it was no more than he deserved. But then with a shrug Nate Ivors was up again and snaking forward, half-bent, until he found the man's shape crumpled against the cold earth. There might be some life in the stupid idiot. Ivors put down his rifle long enough to get hold of an arm and a leg, hoist the man up to his shoulders. Then leaving Bushong's saddle-gun where it lay, he got his own weapon and went hurrying back towards the house, grunting under the burden's considerable weight.

So this was the tally to date, from Ross Boyden's smart scheme to pry Emery out of his hole. One of their own men down! Nate Ivors for one decided he didn't want any more of this.

Wade Emery could have got that second man, easily; but something in the audacity of him—rushing in like that, picking up the body under the very cover of a waiting rifle—made him hold his fire. He had moved from his original position, after those first few bullets that had scared the life out of Boyden, and into another spot chosen in advance—a spot where there would be no chance of getting above him and surrounding him. Boyden, however, had risen to the bait of those first shots and was sending his men up, and from the new position Emery had been able to watch, easily, as the two moved in.

The first of the pair had walked practically into his sights. Now as he held his fire he watched the second one scurry away, crab-like, the body of his fallen companion across his shoulders.

He knew very well who it was attacking him, having recognized the sound of Joel Harris's rifle. But much good it and its telescopic sights would do Ross Boyden in the night, he thought grimly.

Cracking open the new box of shells, he set it on the rock in front of him and fed gleaming cartridges into the rifle. The biting smell of burnt powder was in the chamber, the barrel warm to his wind-chilled hands. He snapped shut the breech, returned the box to his jacket pocket, and got down into position again. Joel Harris's stolen rifle lanced red fire, down where Boyden was hunkered in the shelter of a woodpile, and Wade aimed at it, trying for a hit. He knew it was no good.

And then silence set in. Emery, peering into the tangled starshadows, wished for a moon. He had lost sight of the retreating flanker and his burden, and any movement was lost in the darkness down there beyond the house. There was no sound, either, except the wash of wind through scrub brush and scattered pine.

Hoofbeats began, suddenly. At once Wade Emery was on his feet and emptying his rifle chamber in a series of offhand, rapidly-flung shots. He quit when the dimming pound of the horses told him the men were well out of range. Then he lowered the rifle and stood like that a moment, a thin smile on his tight mouth. That, he figured, was that. . . .

Charlie Rook, lagging behind with Jeff Bushong's horse, cursed softly. "Jeff's dead, Ross!"

"Damn that drifter!" the foreman gritted. And briefly, over his shoulder: "Bring him along, Charlie."

Nate Ivors hipped around for a last look at the dark ranch where they had run into disaster; melting back into the shadows as they left there, it looked again as empty, as deserted, as before that single rifle had begun its leaden song.

"What will you tell Mallard?" he asked pleasantly, turning back to the foreman. "That a lone man drove off the four of us, and converted one into a corpse?"

Boyden did not even look at him. He grunted: "We weren't looking for trouble! I never dreamed that drifter had the guts to stick; but with him forted in the rocks an army couldn't have knocked him out—not by starlight.

"There'll be another time," he added grimly. "We'll know what to expect, after this. And he's in the way, and we're gonna be rid of him. That's a promise!"

CHAPTER VI

When Dick Rudebaugh came along the street in eight o'clock sunshine, to open his office for the day, he found Wade Emery on the courthouse veranda waiting for him. If sight of the drifter surprised him, the sheriff's sharp blue eyes showed none of it. All he said was: "Well. Good morning!" and came up the warped plank steps.

Wade Emery pushed out of the split-bottomed rocker.

"I wanted to see you, Sheriff."

His voice meant trouble. Rudebaugh nodded his shaggy head, jerked a broad thumb towards the door. "C'mon inside," he muttered. With Emery following, he stumped into the dark hallway, used a key on the lock of his office door and kicked the door open. They walked into stale, musty air. Rudebaugh flipped the latches on the windows, ran them wide, and as morning coolness breathed freshly into the room turned to his desk. "Have a chair."

His visitor obeyed, moving stiffly. He held the battered, shapeless hat in both hard hands. The drifter was as shabby, his beard as stubby and untended as yesterday, and he still bore the marks of what the sheriff judged must have been a hell of a fight. Rudebaugh dropped heavily into his swivel chair, dropped hands onto his broad thighs and swung around to face his caller. Bad digestion working on a heavy breakfast produced a rumbling belch; the sheriff growled, "S'cuse me." Then his blue eyes were full on the other and he was saying: "Well, seems to me something was said yesterday about you leaving town."

"I guess there was," Emery agreed.

"Ross Boyden, wasn't it?" the sheriff pursued. "And I thought you had agreed to go."

"I told him I had thought it over," the other corrected him. "I didn't say what conclusion I'd come to."

"Oh." The sheriff belched again. "Damn them sausages!" he muttered. "What's your business, son?"

"Night riders were on the Saddle last night. They hit my boss's place. They had guns and they used them."

The sheriff was scowling, his blue eyes boring into the other man's. "The hell you say! Any damage done?"

"No. I heard them coming and hid out in the brush; they threw some lead at me but I managed to stay out of sight. I thought they were going to torch the buildings, but they didn't."

"You didn't recognize anyone, I suppose?"

Wade hesitated. The sound of the rifle Ross Boyden stole had been recognition enough, but he decided not to bring that into the picture.

"No," he answered. "There wasn't any moon, you know."

The sheriff dragged a hand across heavy cheeks. "A hell of a note!" he muttered. "But you don't give me much to go on."

"No, sir," agreed Emery, meekly. "Still, there ought to be something you can do. You're the law, and you've got my boss under arrest; and it ought to be up to you to protect his property since he can't be around himself to do it. Me—" he shrugged, looking at his cracked boot toes. "I'm no gunslinger; outside of doin' the chores, I'm worse than no help at all. I wasn't signed on to hold off no night riders!"

Dick Rudebaugh glanced at him, sidelong, and then his eyes slid away filled with a faint disgust. He grunted something, and scowled into space as he tapped the arm of his chair with blunt fingers.

Inwardly, Wade Emery was pleased. This was just the effect he had been working for, and now his mission to town was finished. It had been a very unpleasant chore. He had made the call upon the sheriff only because there was always a chance Rudebaugh might learn, indirectly, of the raid on Saddleback and would wonder then why Emery had not come to him about it.

Rudebaugh, for himself, was greatly perturbed by the report of night riders on the Saddle; it outweighed in his mind any interest in this shabby nonentity who had brought the news, and about whom he felt nothing stronger than a vague contempt. Lee Ball had learned nothing from his efforts in trailing the man last night. Emery had gone straight home to Saddleback, with apparently no attempt to recover the loot from the Kingdom payroll hold-up. That meant one thing, in all probability—that Joel Harris had no particular trust for this saddletramp who worked for him and so had merely been disinclined to reveal the hiding-place to him. And yet there was always another possibility: that Harris was actually innocent, in spite of everything Crown had to say.

Wade Emery shifted his feet, stood up. "Well," he grunted, "I told you; that's the most I can do! If the ranch gets burned down the blame is off my shoulders, and I'm gonna tell my boss that!"

"All right—hold on a minute!" The sheriff got up, too, and dragged on his greasy hat with a weary gesture. "No saddletramp's telling me how to run my office!" he growled. "Come along while I get my bronc, and we'll be riding!"

A question was in Emery's mind, as he went with the sheriff. He had left the jughead roan snubbed to the courthouse railing; Wade took it on trailing reins and went along to Rudebaugh's house and private corral where he kept a fine white-stockinged black, at the county's expense. A big-boned gelding, it had speed and bottom and the endurance to carry its owner's build over long trails. The heat was just coming into the day as the two men cantered away from town, past the park and the river.

Wade Emery asked himself what good the sheriff hoped to achieve by riding up to Saddleback himself, so long after the night raid. Then, without explanation, the sheriff turned out of the upward trail into another valley road, and Wade saw that they were not headed for the Saddle at all. He knew now where they were going and it only increased his puzzlement.

Crown ranch headquarters stood at the head of a gentle swell, with good grass, good water, and a fine view of the downward sweep of this mountain valley; Thad Kingdom had chosen the site carefully. The big, two-story house was a dazzle of white in morning sunshine, behind its border of straight, upward-reaching poplars that moved gracefully in an early breeze. Stately pillars marched across the building's front, and a drive looped before it across green lawns. The corrals, barns, bunkhouses, lay in back, and slightly under the crest of the hill, so that as one approached they did not mar the aristocratic appearance of this cattleman's mansion.

On the green lawn before the house a raven-haired girl was teaching her paint pony to do a trick. She looked up as she heard Wade and the sheriff coming; she waved and called, "Hello,

Dick!" and leading the pony walked over to meet them as they reined in.

"Well, Lynne," said the sheriff.

Wade looked at her with open interest. She was a small girl, but with an outdoor sturdiness about her. The rounded arms, the oval face, the delicately modelled throat revealed by the unbuttoned collar of the yellow silk shirt, had a lustre of golden tan that meant sun and wind and vibrant health. The riding clothes she wore were expensive ones; her manner showed that she was accustomed and familiar with expensive things. Her wide, clear brow, the brown eyes, the full and merry lips were those of a girl who had never been crossed in life; but there was a hint of the stubbornness she had inherited from old Thad Kingdom, and which a reversal of fortune might someday bring out in a flashing of the eyes and a hardening of the firm but rounded chin.

Looking at this girl whom he had never seen but of whom he had heard so much from Joel Harris, Wade knew no difficulty in understanding what it was about her that had taken his friend's eye. She in turn met his look, frankly, and obviously not impressed by what she saw. A quick glance over the bearded face, the worn clothing, and she passed him up and returned her attention to the sheriff. "Out early, Dick?"

"Yeah," he admitted, nodding his big shaggy head. "Early for me." He looked at the paint pony. "How's Prince coming along with his education?"

"Just look!" she cried. She stepped back, to the horse's head, gave his knee a light tap with the short riding quirt she carried, and at once Prince bent the knee and went down upon it, his handsome head dipping in a graceful bow. Lynne Kingdom laughed gaily, slapped the sleek bright neck; and Prince came up again with a flirt of tail and mane, and did a few prancing steps with head bobbing. And then he came to her and nuzzled her palm for the sugar she held out as reward.

Sheriff Rudebaugh grunted. "Dunno what good it'll do him," he said, "except to get a bait of sugar. Still, I guess it's all right."

"Oh, you're just jealous! Because Stockings can't do tricks."

"This animal?" echoed the sheriff, abashed. He slapped the black's shoulder with a calloused hand. He grinned. "No thanks, ma'am! Stockin's has to work for a living."

He turned serious, then. "I'd like to see your dad if I can. That's what we rode out for."

This brought the unshaven drifter into the conversation, and Wade Emery could read in the girl's eyes a sudden question as to what business her father could have with such a man. But she said, simply: "Why, of course, Dick. I think he's in the office."

Rudebaugh jerked his head at Wade and they rode on around the side of the house, leaving the girl staring after them with vague puzzlement tugging at her brow. Near the kitchen lean-to there was a gnawed hitchpole and a water tank, and the sheriff dismounted here and the other man followed suit. At a call from Rudebaugh curtains were drawn aside at a window of the lower story and Thad Kingdom's face showed. The old man said shortly: "What is it?"

"Got to talk business, Thad," said Rudebaugh. "We're coming in."

They went through a side door and into the rancher's study. Like Kingdom, like his house and his person, the place was scrupulously tidy—a sharp contrast to the sheriff's littered office in town. A rack full of guns shone and gleamed in one corner; a deer head thrust out from the wall opposite the neat and barren desk. A rag rug was on the floor. Even in his own house, Thad Kingdom could not relax; he sat stiff and straight in a hard-backed chair at the desk, turned towards the door and frowning darkly as Rudebaugh and his companion entered.

"Why do you bring this man here, Rudebaugh?" he demanded bluntly.

"I got my reasons!" the sheriff answered; and since the rancher made no move towards hospitality, he shrugged and dropped into an upholstered chair under the deer head. He said to

Emery, "Take a seat." But Wade Emery remained standing, not liking this.

"Thad," began the sheriff, abruptly. "Where was your crew last night?"

A stony mask dropped over the thin, seamed face. "That's a damned funny question!"

"Night riders were up to the Saddle," Rudebaugh went on, watching his blunt hand as it fingered a frayed edge of his vest. "The fellow here says they raided the Harris place. I'd just like to find out if you had anything to do with it."

The blue-veined lids slid down until they almost covered the slitted brown eyes. Thad Kingdom's thin hand lifted from the desk beside him and he pointed at the door. He said tightly: "Get out!"

Dick Rudebaugh made no move. He said: "You put me on a spot, Thad, with that injunction. Now the least you can do in return is to be frank with me. I'll take a yes or no answer, but I won't take that daughter-into-the-snow gesture. And don't act like I'm insultin' you, either—because I know damn well you ain't above doing a thing like what happened last night if it occurred to you, or would stand to do you any good. How else do I suppose you came to be top dog on this range, anyway?

"Now there's at least a good chance," he went on evenly, ignoring the thunder piling up behind the rancher's stiff features, "that you ordered that raid on the Harris place. I won't bother to name my reasons for thinking so, because they're a bit personal. But I dunno what good it'd do you to lie about it!"

There was a silence of fierce intensity. Old Kingdom swallowed, the muscles cording in his scrawny, turkey neck. His voice trembled a little when he spoke: "I could have you hounded out of office for this, Sheriff. I've never let any man talk to me the way you're doing!"

Rudebaugh stirred heavy shoulders, shook his shaggy head a little. "You ain't apt to do anything to me. You know I'm honest, and you know you can push damn dirty chores off onto me—such as that injunction—and that I'll take it because I try to do a job. The least you can expect to get in return is some frank talk."

"All right." Kingdom had calmed again, but his tone was still icy. "Your answer is—no! Crown had nothing to do with last night; there's nothing about that jailbird's spread up there to be of the slightest interest to me. Now—go on from there, any direction you like."

"I will." Dick Rudebaugh pushed to his feet. "Looks like the next stop is Bar M. Thanks for the trouble, Thad. And I reckon I'll take your word, all right."

Wade pushed away from the wall where he had leaned, watching the scene. The old rancher's keen glance swung to him, coldly. He said to the sheriff: "Did you get that stolen money out of him, Rudebaugh?"

"Nope. I'm still working on that." Rudebaugh jerked his head at the drifter. "Let's go."

"Just a minute!" At Emery's suddenly sharp tone they both looked at him. "I reckon I deserve to know the answer to one question, since I'm being brought into this robbery business."

"Yeah?" said Rudebaugh. "What is it?"

"If the man that lifted the payroll was masked, then just how, Mr. Kingdom, did you happen to recognize him?"

The rancher's white brows dragged down. "As a matter of fact," he grunted, "I didn't. He stayed in the brush while I threw the money to him. But one of my riders, Bart Yaeger, was with me and he got a good look at Harris's clothing, and the bronc he was forking."

"Sure," growled Rudebaugh. "I could have told you all that, if you'd asked me, son."

Emery said: "Okay, I reckon I got my answer. . . ."

They mounted, and they rode away. Wade found himself hunting for another glimpse of the girl and the pony, but in vain. Then they had left the big white house shining on its hill, with the poplars singing around it and the grassy slope spreading away before.

Where the trail branched into the main valley road, Rudebaugh pulled in and squinted at the lift of the Saddle, and at the fleecy clouds touching Baldy's bright brow, and he looked at Wade. "That's a long ride across the pass to Bar M," he muttered, scowling. "Steve Mallard's bound to be in town today or tomorrow, or if he don't make it I'll plan to take the ride over the slope and talk to him. Can't work it in right now." He added: "Lemme know if you have any more trouble, won't you?"

Emery shrugged. He had already wasted a good part of the morning tagging after the sheriff, and he was as pleased to call this off. Remembering the role he was playing, he said: "Don't make no difference to me what you do— because if they come again I'm not staying to meet them! It ain't worth my neck. I'll take my horse and light a shuck clean out of this damn country."

The sheriff only grunted, as though it were the sort of statement he might have expected from this drifter; and Wade Emery was pleased to let him think that. But next moment he surprised the sheriff. He added: "By the way, that gent you put to follow me home from town last evening made me kind of nervous. I hope you won't be sending him again."

Dick Rudebaugh dropped his eyes quickly, rather taken aback. "Damn that Lee Ball!" he muttered. "I told him to be careful." He shrugged. "Well, I wanted to prove a hunch about you, was all. What Lee had to report satisfied me. He won't bother you any more."

"Thanks," grunted Wade Emery, drily. He looked at the high sun, dragged his battered hat on farther. "Well, I got chores. I better be heading for Saddleback."

They parted there at the fork in the road, Wade heading towards the broad notch that the Saddle made into the line of timbered hills. He was troubled by the sheriff's last remark, wondering what "hunch" Rudebaugh had proved about him. At that moment, he would have been even more alarmed could he have read the sheriff's thoughts.

For Dick Rudebaugh, heavy in the saddle, was waiting back there at the fork and frowning at the dust plume the vanishing rider trailed behind him across the swells of bunch grass and sage. And Rudebaugh was muttering, with a tone of dissatisfaction: "I dunno. More I see of that gent, the more I wonder. He ain't just what he wants me to think he is. There's something wrong there—something phony!"

CHAPTER VII

For some time after his visitors had gone, Thad Kingdom sat very quietly except for the nervous drumming of thin fingers against the polished desk-top. A peculiar expression had come into his face—a look of doubt and uncertainty that put bafflement into the faded brown eyes. Then he caught sight of his foreman crossing the ranch yard and half-rising from his chair called to him across the window-sill. "Short! Come in here!"

Chuck Short recognized an unfamiliar tone in the summons, but he took his time about obeying it. That, he had found by long experience, was the best way to deal with Thad Kingdom—giving him back a certain amount of audacity, as token of his lack of fear for his boss.

Presently he slouched into the office, heavy-lidded eyes placid, the hat with its whang-leathered brim shoved back from brown, high forehead. He said, "Yeah?"

Kingdom, with both hands gripping the arms of his chair, demanded bluntly: "You wouldn't doublecross me, would you?"

A hard light flickered in the heavy eyes; the slackness ran out of Short's loose-hung body. He said again: "Yeah?"

"Someone took guns up to the Harris place last night. Was it you—in spite of my orders to stay away from there? Damn it, I want to know!"

Short made a small gesture. He did not answer. He said instead, shrewdly: "Somebody told me the sheriff came around this morning. What happened? He gave you some nasty talk—so you're taking it out on me?"

"Never mind that!" growled Kingdom. "The point is I gave definite orders that Harris was to be left alone!"

"That was after you changed your tune," the foreman pointed out drily. "Before, you was full of running the guy out of the country. You went soft awful quick!"

The rancher came out of his chair, taut with anger. "Don't talk to me that way, you scum!" he thundered. The light leaped again behind Short's heavy-lidded eyes. Kingdom did not appear to notice. He had overcome that moment of anger, regained his aristocratic calm. He went on, more quietly: "Much as I dislike having that jailbird on the Saddle, I figure it's better with him there than not. You're to leave him alone!"

Chuck Short said: "Maybe you forgot. He's going back to the pen—for robbery."

The old man's mouth tightened on a hard decision. He said: "I've just been thinking it over. I may decide to drop the charges; to let him keep the money he stole from me, if I have to!"

"But for the love of God!" the foreman blurted. "Why?"

"Because," Kingdom said, resignedly, "him being located up there in the Saddle acts as a buffer between this west slope and the east. I don't mind admitting it, Short; I'm afraid of Steve Mallard!"

For a moment nothing was said, as Chuck Short stared at him, digesting this. Thad Kingdom—afraid!

"It come on me in the middle of the night," Thad went on, heavily—"I thought I pulled a smart move, yesterday, with that injunction. Now I'm not so sure. I'm an old man, Chuck. I've fought my wars. I—I don't know whether I can fight another through, or not!"

He turned away from his foreman, and pain was in his eyes as he looked through the window, out across the corrals and buildings and, beyond that, the broad acres of this ranch of his, and the farther lift of pine-clad hills.

Chuck Short said then, slowly: "Well, it looks like your war had begun, Thad. Because it sure wasn't me or any of my men that raided Saddleback. It could only have been Mallard!"

He saw the straight back stiffen. Thad Kingdom turned, his face again hard and impassive, the tiredness gone from it suddenly; the stubbornness back in the set of the jaw. He said: "All right! If it's war, I promise Crown will hold up its end;

and we won't hide behind the law, either. Short, I want you to station a look-out, day and night, up yonder at that slide. I want brush piled there, ready to be fired as a signal at any moment that Mallard makes a move to try his dynamite. We'll wait for the signal—whether smoke by day, or flame by night—and when it comes we'll be up there before he knows what's hit him. If he thinks it's going to be an easy matter, setting off the blast that will ruin Kingdom range, he'll find how mistaken he is!

"Go post that guard, Short. Right away!"

"Yeah!"

Chuck Short touched his hat brim briefly, turned and strode out of the house in a jingling of spur chains. With the side door swung to behind him, he stood in the full blast of the morning sun that was beginning already to take on heat, and his face was a hard mask as he thought over what he had learned.

He had been foreman for Crown eight years, now. It had been a good job, despite Kingdom's tempers and his supercilious, aristocratic notions. But now, a chill warning began to work along his spine. There could be an end to everything. And if you saw a ship was leaking, it was better to get off before she went down with you. . . .

A cowhand came trailing through the yard and Short hailed him. "I got a job for you," he ordered. "Get your blankets, and have the cook put up some food. You're going into the hills for a couple of days." He told the man about the lookout Thad Kingdom wanted, and its purpose. He added: "If you see Al Briscoe, take him along—two will be better on a lonely job like that. And I'll send up a relief tomorrow night."

The man said "Okay," a little surlily, and headed for the bunkhouse; and Short went back to his sober thoughts. If you're going to make a break, he told himself, you'll have to make it now and make it clean. It was all at once a matter of picking the winning side, and placing his bets accordingly. He had much to offer—enough to make him welcome if he decided to sell out to Steve Mallard.

Lynne Kingdom came from the barn, slapping idly at booted ankles with the riding-crop in her firm, brown hand. Her glance crossed Short's; she looked away quickly, with a toss of glossy black curls. The foreman's lantern jaw hardened.

Damned, stuck-up wench! He was thinking of the night, not many months ago, when he had felt that riding-crop laid sharply across his cheek; and the sting of the blow came back so strongly that he raised one hand and touched the place, remembering. All because he tried to kiss her! True, he had been a little drunk, and woman-hungry. But he hadn't hurt her any, and the kiss itself was nothing. It was him touching her—him thinking himself good enough to place himself

83

on a common level with her: that's why she had struck, and she had struck hard, and left him staggering there with hot anger quenching the passion that had risen, dumbly, within him.

She had never mentioned the occurrence to her father, he had to say that much for her; otherwise Chuck Short would have been fired on the spot, even after all his years of service to Crown. But though she kept the incident to herself, she had never since that day made any attempt to conceal her loathing and contempt for her father's foreman. And however well he served the family and the ranch, he would never be good enough, in the girl's eyes, at least, to touch the buckle of her boot, the skirt of her saddle. . . .

Suddenly then he found his decision formed. He stepped down from the doorway, went across the yard. The puncher detailed for the look-out, up on the slide, came from the bunkhouse with certain belongings and laid them by the door, started to go to the cookshed. Chuck Short halted him. "Bart Yaeger left yet, do you know?"

He had sent Yaeger to mend some fence along a vega in the lower range. The puncher told him: "Yeah. An hour ago, I reckon."

"Thanks."

Chuck Short's favourite saddler was a grey—an ugly-tempered brute; master and mount understood each other perfectly. Short roped it out of the horse-lot, threw on blanket and saddle and cinched up with no gentle hand. As he found stirrup and settled into leather, the brute swung its head back and tried to bite his leg with its long, yellow teeth. Short gave the beast a kick in the jaw.

They left the ranch headquarters behind them, struck out at a rolling lope across rich bottom-lands thick with cattle bearing the pronged Crown burn. Any trace of morning coolness had left the air by now. The sun had its familiar breathless weight. But there was a haze high against the western sky that might mean rain was coming in. It should mean that. This range was overdue.

He spotted Bart Yaeger by the wagon and team he had brought out with him, loaded with new wire and wire stretcher and boxes of staples and new-cut posts. The man was working with a post hole digger, bent over the work and sweating and mad. When he heard Short's bronc nearing and straightened up, sleeving sweat from his red and sullen face, an habitual stoop remained in Yaeger's narrow shoulders.

"Howdy," he grunted.

Short reined in and eased around in saddle for a look at the job Yaeger was doing. The posts of the original fence had not been creosoted when they were set in, and with time had rotted off in the ground. Then cattle had broken down the fence and got into the vega, into the thick grass

Crown was saving to cut for winter hay. It was Bart Yaeger's job to dig new holes, plant new posts and string new wire.

Chuck Short swung down, snubbed his reins to a wheel of the wagon and moved in to give Yaeger a hand. They worked a while like that in silence, only giving vent to an occasional grunt or swear word as a pole gave them trouble or the wire stretcher slipped.

Presently the foreman put down his tools, stepped away and surveyed the work that had been done, as he rolled a smoke with makings from his pocket. Over the twisting of the paper he remarked then, quite casually: "How long you been on Mallard's payroll, Bart?"

Yaeger swung his head around slowly, favoured Short with a look that was as near to wooden as a man's face can assume. Short did not wait for an answer. He stuck the quirly between thin lips, wiped a match aflame against lifted thigh and brought it up behind cupped hands. Shaking out the match then, the cigarette bobbing in his mouth as he spoke and the blue smoke of it trailing up into a squinted eye, he observed: "I'm considering makin' a change. About fed-up with the Kingdoms. There's greener pastures."

No expression in his stolid face, Bart Yaeger demanded flatly: "What gave you the idea there's anything between me and Mallard?"

The other shrugged, picked the cigarette from

between his lips and studied the burning of it. He returned it. "Number of things. You identified this Harris gent, at the stick-up yesterday, and it was you shot him out of the saddle. Now, I understand, Bar M has made a raid on Saddleback during the night. As Kingdom says, Harris was a buffer between the two slopes. Looks like Mallard is working to get him out of the way—and that maybe you were helping him with a frame-up."

He looked at Yaeger then, and Yaeger had a gun in his hand. Short had not seen the draw, but the gun was there and the muzzle of it was a black menace trained straight at the foreman's belt buckle. Yaeger said: "Maybe you think I won't work the trigger on this thing?"

"Put it away!" growled Short, on a tone of disgust. "Can't a man talk plain without you getting proddy? I ain't gonna blab to old man Kingdom. I figure I'm about through with him—him and Crown too. They're worn out, and they're washed-up. They've had their way of things too long.

"Bar M, on the other hand, has got its back to the wall, and that means it'll fight. And Steve Mallard is a young man, with ideas. I like a gent like that. And I think I got information he can use."

He paused. No shadow of thought had flickered across Yaeger's face as Short was speaking, but slowly the hand holding the Colt had dragged downward as though pulled by the gun's weight, until the arm hung loosely at the man's side. That was as much answer as Chuck needed. So he said now: "I want to talk to Mallard, but I want to do it without anyone from this side knowing. How can that be managed?"

"Steve expects to be in town tomorrow afternoon," Bart Yaeger grunted finally, his eyes carefully following the flight of a meadow-lark as it took off, suddenly, from the deep and swaying grass of the vega. "Go to Phil Nolan's store. He has a back room where I've been contacting men from Bar M. Tell them I said it was all right."

Chuck Short nodded, brusquely. "Thanks." He took the cigarette from his mouth, tossed it away. He went to his horse and jerked reins free of the wagon wheel and stepped up to saddle. Bart Yaeger made no move, said nothing. Short reined around to face him again. "By the way," he said. "That hold-up yesterday—I guessed right, didn't I? It wasn't Harris?"

Yaeger made a brief nod. "It was Jeff Bushong. We saw Harris leave town just a little while before me and Kingdom started out. Steve Mallard cooked up the idea on the spur of the moment. When I said I recognized Harris, old Kingdom was ready enough to believe me."

"I thought it was like that. . . . Well, see you later."

As Short kicked with his spurs and the grey took him away from there, he looked back to see the thick, hump-shouldered figure of Yaeger standing with a raw post hole gaping at his feet, his eyes watching the disappearing rider.

CHAPTER VIII

The storm came in with evening, on a massive flotilla of thunderheads that swept up from the west and the distant ocean. Here on the high perch of the Saddle, Wade Emery could look down upon those clouds; could see the white brilliance of the foamy crests creaming against the incredible blue of the sky, and see at the same time the dark underbelly of the cloud mass with the angry flicker of lightning shooting through it. Grandly the clouds moved in, bringing the smell of rain, spreading their shadow like a blanket over the roll and dip of the foothills until at last they rolled against the great wall of the hills and broke there. And then the storm broke too.

It had been a busy day for Emery, hurrying to catch up with the work of the spread before the oncoming storm overtook him. When it came he was ready for it, and he sat alone in the shack listening to the pelting of the rain as it marched in sheets across the heights, and the thunder crashed among the peaks and lightning made its eye-punishing glare.

This, he knew, would be a grateful blessing to the summer-parched range; he could picture in his mind's eye the little town in the valley below, its streets turned to mud, rain washing the windows of Joel Harris's room, sweeping against the high cupola of the courthouse, dappling the surface of the river in the park. But he knew at the same time that Steve Mallard's Bar M would get very little benefit from the storm, for his range lay in the rain-shadow of these mountains. To men of the dry eastern slope, the storm's fury would be nothing but a piling of clouds and a flicker of lightning seen off against the jagged skyline, and perhaps a dimly heard muttering of thunder. It must be a bitter mockery, indeed.

But at least Bar M would not be raiding tonight; there was that much satisfaction for the shabby, lonely man keeping his vigil in the shack on the mountain ranch. He was dead tired, for there had been little sleep last night even when he felt certain Ross Boyden did not intend returning after the fiasco of the first raid on Saddleback.

Emery cooked and ate his supper, cleaned up after himself, and straightened out the cabin. He went and stood in the door awhile after that, letting the chill rain wind beat against him and looking out at the storm while he smoked a pipeful of his diminishing supply of tobacco. He had many things to think about; but when, at the last he found his thoughts turning unbidden to the girl he had seen that morning—Lynne Kingdom, of the lustrous dark curls and merry laugh—he grunted impatiently at himself and went back inside the cabin, knocking out his pipe against the door and letting the wind carry the sparks away in a long red stream, to be lost in the beat of the storm.

When he awoke next morning the sky was washed clean and rocks steamed under the warm sun. Wade Emery, on an impulse born of his speculations last night, caught up the jughead about ten o'clock and headed it across the Saddle, putting it at the steep face of the rise that built up towards old Baldy's bleak flanks.

This was tough climbing. At one place there was the roar and plunge of a waterfall, the foot of it lost in spray that had a rainbow woven through. Lower down, the water that tumbled over this cataract became the principal stream threading Thad Kingdom's range. Soaked with flying spray, his bronc slipping on moss-grown boulders, Emery got above this falls, went higher to where the torrent became a mere trickle against the barren rock. At last he found the thing that he had made this climb to see.

Months ago, some frost-split fissure had given way and caused a tiny spill of rubble. This had grown, taking on momentum and size, until in the end a great dust-raising slide had gone thundering down one of these high mountain gorges. There, before Wade Emery now, was the result—a long, tapering ridge of boulders piled up, some of them larger than the shack on Saddleback. It stretched in an ugly scar down the face of a barren slant, and at the foot of this it backed up in a great heaping that completely blocked what had once been a natural watershed.

Westward of this block, the rocks were moist with the running of many little streams that sprang forth here from subterranean sources. To the east there were, instead, only the unmistakable marks where water had once flowed, but where now there was no water. This, then, was the source of Bar M's troubles, and the cause of the crisis that had gripped both slopes of this high spine of hills—and the Saddle that lay between.

Over all lay the dead silence of the heights.

Wade Emery was urging his bronc forward over the uncertain footing, studying the scene with careful, frowning eyes, when a sharp voice across the thin, high air cut in on his thoughts. "Don't come any closer! Rein in and put your hands high until we look you over!"

Startled, Wade Emery moved to obey, while he sought to locate the direction of that unexpected voice. Then he saw a glint of sunlight on metal, and turning that way caught sight of a shadowed hollow under the lip of a shallow ledge of rock, and the scrub growth clinging to the grey, weathered surface of the cliff. There were blankets that looked soaked, as though the storm last night had had its way with them. A coffee-pot sat slantwise on a small and smoking fire. There were two men, in the protection of a boulder resting before the campsite, and the one who had spoken said: "Check him for a gun, Al." To Wade he added, in warning: "We had a damn wet night of it. My trigger finger's still begging for trouble. So take it awful easy!"

They looked short-tempered and suspicious, their faces blue and pinched from the misery of the night. The one called Al came out and moved cautiously towards Emery across the sun-steaming ground. He pawed over the prisoner's clothing, stepped back. "Nothing on him."

"Step down from saddle," the other commanded. "You can put your arms down but do it careful." Moving out beside his companion, while Emery was obeying this order, he asked Al: "Ever see the guy before? Looks like a damn saddletramp to me."

"What's your business up here?" Al demanded, eyes studying the prisoner narrowly. "Better make it sound good."

"I guess I haven't any business," Wade admitted. "I wanted to take a look at the slide I'd heard so much about. Just curious, I guess."

The man with the gun mimicked, with twisted mouth: "Just curious!" He looked at Al. "Short never gave no instructions for a thing like this."

Wade Emery caught the name quickly. "Short? Are you Crown?"

Al was scowling. "What if we are?" He added: "I'm gonna take a look in his saddle-pockets.

If I find any powder or cord it'll go hard for him."

"Sure," said Emery. "You'll find nothing. Mallard never sent me up here."

The saddle-pockets proving empty put a perplexed frown in Al's face. "I dunno," he muttered. "Dunno what we should do with you. Wouldn't feel easy, just turning you loose around that slide—"

A sudden exclamation from the second Crown man interrupted him: "Hey, look—someone else coming!"

In their interest in Wade Emery they had let this other rider come almost upon them without noticing. All three recognized Lynne Kingdom, at once. She looked just as Wade had seen her yesterday—just as warm, just as calmly sure of herself and her world. She was mounted on a big, rawboned sorrel. Seeing the two Kingdom riders she showed surprise, and exclaimed: "Well, Al—and Sid! What are you boys doing here?" Looking at Wade, her clear brow bunched a little. She remembered him, from yesterday. She said: "And what's this you've got?"

"It's your dad's orders, Miss Kingdom," Al explained, and told the purpose of their vigil. "No knowing who you're apt to find snooping around this slide," he pointed out. "We caught this one just a minute ago. Refuses to say who he is or what he wants."

"On the contrary," Emery put in, quietly. "I haven't refused to tell them anything. They didn't ask who I was—only what I wanted, and I honestly said I was up here out of curiosity. That's the reason you came, isn't it?"

Lynne Kingdom turned her glance upon him, and she was frowning. "Supposing it is," she said. "What's your name?"

"Wade Emery. I'm Joel Harris's hired man."

Her naturally arched brows went up, new interest coming into her brown eyes. "Joel—?"

"Now I know I don't trust this jigger!" grunted the man called Al. "Not after what his boss did—"

Lynne turned on him. "What are you talking about?"

"You mean," Wade Emery said, sharply, "you hadn't heard about day before yesterday?"

"Why, not a word—" Her expression was frankly puzzled.

Sid made a wry face. "Well, the cat's out of the bag now! Miss Kingdom, Al's talking about this Harris gent holding up your dad and Bart Yaeger, and lifting the payroll!"

"Only it's not true," Wade Emery said quickly. "Yaeger made a mistake—or told a lie—"

Lynne was staring at him. "But you say this happened two days ago?"

"Yes. Apparently," Wade added, drily, "your father has passed the order among his hands to keep the news away from you. For some reason he would rather you didn't hear."

"Where is Joel now? I came by Saddleback, on my way up here. It looked deserted."

"It is, all but for me. My boss is at the doctor's house in town, under arrest. He was shot. Not seriously," he added, quickly.

Lynne Kingdom's face had gone white. She glanced at the jughead roan and told Wade: "If that's your horse, better mount him and come with me."

One of the Crown riders started to protest, then thought better of it. Silence dropped over them as Emery went to his bronc and swung up to saddle.

They took the difficult drop away from that high place with little talk, for it was hard to speak with their horses manoeuvring the steep footing. Once Lynne threw out an arm to point. "What do you suppose that is?"

Wade saw a huge pile of brush, stacked high upon a flat rock table. The place was exposed, the cliff falling away sharply before it. He thought he knew, suddenly, what its purpose was. "It must be the signal," he suggested. "Put a light to that and it could be seen pretty far across the valley."

It was a wide view they had, from this point. The girl murmured: "It's beautiful—too beautiful for the trouble that's come here."

He only nodded in agreement.

They came down, slowly; past the waterfall,

98

where Lynne Kingdom remarked the rainbow colours that lived in the mist boiling at its foot. They stopped here a moment, sitting saddle to look upon the slide and plunge of the water, to feel the spray of it blowing cold against their faces. Then down again, over slippery rocks, until at last they reached the gentle slope of the Saddle and Lynne dismounted, to let her sorrel rest briefly.

Wade swung down also. He said: "Thanks for taking me away from those two Crown men. I'm afraid their tempers were a little short."

"Yes," she said.

Standing there close beside her, in morning sunlight, with their broncs pulling at the sparse grass of the Saddle and the green and silver of the valley opening at their feet, his thoughts were full of this girl. It was not alone the physical pull of her attraction, though this was strong enough to make itself felt in strange, troubling emotions such as the drifter—nameless, homeless, without past or hope of future—had seldom known to be roused at the mere sight of a woman. For there was the promise of other qualities—a steadiness, a clearness of vision, an essential honesty.

Then he asked himself: why not? What more natural for a girl who had everything, who in her short life had never known the toil and despair that, for example, had fined down Terry Franz and taken away from the doctor's daughter all girlish joy of life that was her right? And yet, with the next breath, he countered this argument. Her father's wealth could not be counted against Lynne Kingdom. And there was something about her which suggested that, in a crisis, latent qualities would manifest themselves in this girl which, up to now, there had been nothing to call forth.

She cut in upon his thoughts. She said, frowning: "Poor Joel. . . . Wade, you're his friend, aren't you?"

"Yes." She had turned towards him, head tilted, brown eyes searching his with a direct intentness. The man said: "He asked me to find out what you knew of all this, and what you thought."

"Is he—bitter?"

"A little, I'm afraid. He even thinks your father lied, to saddle him with this crime. I know now, of course, that that isn't true, for otherwise your father would never have kept the news of the hold-up from you. He'd have told you, and gloated over the proof that Joel Harris was no good."

Something in the quality of her glance stopped him, made him frown in some confusion. And then he heard her saying: "You're a very strange person, Wade Emery! Your dress, your appearance, say one thing—but there's nothing of that in the way you talk. You don't sound like an ignorant saddletramp; why do you permit yourself to look

100

like one? No—" Suddenly, before he knew what she was about, she had moved towards him and putting up both her hands she covered the lower part of his face with them, covered the unsightly stubble of beard. Then only his eyes, pale and blue, were visible above them; and looking into his eyes she exclaimed: "Now I know for sure. The eyes give you away. They don't even belong with the rest of your face. This is just a part you play—"

The nearness of her, the touch of her hands, worked a magic then against which Wade Emery found himself suddenly powerless. Somehow his arms were about her slim waist, tightening; blindly his mouth was coming down upon hers, finding her moist warm lips, crushing them.

For an instant, only. Then with surprising strength the hands dropped to his chest and she was pushing against him, and he released her and went stumbling back. As through a haze of blindness he saw her angry eyes, the fury in every line of her body. "Perhaps I was wrong!" she cried. "You're just exactly what you pretend to be!" The riding-crop hung from her wrist by a looped thong; she flicked her arm, caught the little whip into firm brown fingers. "I've used this on other men like you," she exclaimed. "There are many of them—so many!"

He shook his head, trying to find words; but there were none that would be of any service. He waited, ready to take the blow if she wanted to deliver it. But then Lynne Kingdom had turned quickly and, running to her horse, found the stirrup and swung lithely up into the saddle. From there she looked back at him, and the scorn was a fire that lit her eyes.

"It was my own fault," she said, flatly and bitterly. "Considering the kind of man you are, I got exactly what I should have expected. The normal male reaction!"

She slapped in spurs, and quickly the drum of her sorrel's hoofs were dimming on the valley trail. Even after she had gone, Wade Emery could not discover any words that would have been worth the speaking.

CHAPTER IX

The town dozed in noontime heat. A pigeon or two fluttered around the cupola of the wooden courthouse. The trees of the park lifted, green and refreshed by last night's rain. The clocks in the watchmaker's window ticked together, in ragged chorus, and from the dark interior a grandfather's clock bonged out a single stroke. A few saddle horses and rigs lined the streets. There was not much life.

A paint pony took its rider down one of the narrow side ways that cut across Main Street, and stopped before the sagging picket fence that circled the barren yard and rundown house of Doctor William Franz. The gate with one hinge made a scraping sound, and the porch floor sagged under quick steps. For some moments there was no answer to the knock on the door, and then the doctor himself opened it.

He was a small, thin man, with scraggly muttonchop whiskers and a lost look in the weak blue eyes. In his shirtsleeves, tie undone, he blinked at the caller for a second or two. He said then, with exaggerated dignity: "Yes?"

"I want to talk to Joel Harris," Lynne Kingdom told him.

He only stared, and she thought he swayed

a little. Then he said again, foolishly: "Yes?"

Impatience touched her, but she tried not to let it show. She knew about this man—about the unfortunate turn he had taken upon the death of his wife four years ago. She knew only pity for him, and she said now with no change of tone: "Please! I know Joel is here, and I know he would want to see me."

Then Terry Franz appeared. She took a hold of her father's arm and without any difficulty got him turned away from the door, and he wandered off somewhere. Terry said, in a voice that shook a little: "Please come in, Miss Kingdom. I'm sorry. Pop isn't—feeling well."

"Of course," replied Lynne, quickly.

In Joel's room, the doctor's two smaller children, one on either side of the bed, were watching in fascination while the patient's nimble fingers worked with an old, bone-handled knife and a slab of pinewood. It was something to see the way his face lighted at sight of Thad Kingdom's daughter in the doorway. Terry saw, and there was a dullness in her voice as she told Jim and Chris: "You kids clear out now. Joel's got company."

They were quiet, good-mannered children. They went without a murmur, and their sister followed. At the door she turned long enough to see Lynne Kingdom hurry to the bed and go down on her knees beside it, and take one of Joel's big, work-scarred hands in both of hers. Terry Franz didn't want to see any more.

"... I'm glad you came, Lynne. I was beginning to think that maybe—"

"That maybe I believed what they say about you? Of course I don't. I didn't even know about it until this morning, believe me!" She hesitated. "You were shot?"

He nodded. "In the knee. Doc Franz has done good work fixing it up. You know, he's still a good doctor, when he leaves the bottle alone." Then, as he saw the pain that had come into her lovely brown eyes: "Oh, don't take it so hard, Lynne! I'm a long way from dead."

"But what will happen, Joel? Have you any chance to prove your innocence?"

He looked down at the firm brown hand that held his own, turned it over, caressed the knuckles with his broad thumb. "Not too much!" he said, and his face dropped back into its old hard lines. "I guess I shouldn't mind where I'm going. I've had one shot of prison already. I ought to begin to get used to it!"

"Oh, Joel!" Her voice was unhappy. "It makes me sad to see that in you—that bitterness!"

"I'm sorry. I'm not the kind that can take life's knocks calmly. Like Wade Emery, for example."

He didn't notice how she stiffened at that name, how remembered anger touched her dark eyes. But she would not say anything against

Emery, because Joel lay there trusting his friend. She thought: It's the only thing he has to tie to. It would be too cruel, destroying that trust.

She said: "Joel, if my father sends you to prison on this charge, I'll never forgive him—or myself! Because it's really my fault. He wouldn't be so harshly set against you, except it has infuriated him that you and I should be friends."

"He isn't really to blame, I suppose, seeing the kind of man he is—"

They talked a little longer, and then she stood up lightly and smiled down gently at him. "I have to be going now. But I'll be in again to see you. And you won't let things get too much for you— promise!"

Joel managed to smile, a little, and it lifted the bitter lines from about his eyes and mouth and made him darkly handsome, there against the white of the sheets and pillows. Sunlight from the window lay in a bright square upon the counterpane, upon his big-knuckled hands and the knife and the pine slab and the shavings scattered across his knees.

Lynne left, with a friendly squeezing of his hand. They did not kiss—the thing that was between them had never reached that point, whatever old Thad Kingdom might suppose in his dark imaginings. Lynne Kingdom went out of the bedroom and, seeing nothing of the other occupants, let herself out of the house and closed the warped front door carefully behind her.

Terry Franz, in the kitchen, heard her going. Terry was alone there. She had sent the children outdoors and now that the murmur of voices from Joel's room had ended there was no sound at all in the house and Terry sat alone at the kitchen table, her arms on the clean, threadbare cloth, her head down upon them, sobbing.

The touch of a hand on her shoulder made her sit up startled, but it was only her father. His weak blue eyes showing full of concern, he said: "Why, what's the matter, baby?"

She shrugged, angry with herself. "Nothing, Pop. Nothing." She tried to smile, and used the hem of her apron to wipe the tears from her thin cheeks.

But he would not be put off. "Of course there was something!" He stood looking down at her, one hand tugging at scraggly muttonchop whiskers. He studied the handkerchief tied around her yellow hair, the shapeless mended dress. Then suddenly he remembered the girl who had come to the door. Lynne Kingdom in the fancy, expensive clothes old Thad showered on her. He thought he understood then. By God, there wasn't a girl on this range any better than his Theresa!

He said: "Baby, I just happened to think. You haven't had a new dress since I can remember. Why don't you go down to Nolan's and—?"

107

His voice faded out under her look—the indulgent, head-shaking smile one gives a child's fine, impractical dreams. "You know we can't afford it, Pop!" There was no reproach in her voice, for she was thinking with a wry twist of amusement how far he was from guessing the true reason for her tears. But there was self-reproach in the look that came across the doctor as he heard, and saw her face.

"No we can't!" he admitted. "And I guess I know whose fault it is, too. I swear I don't see why you put up with a damn, drunken—"

"Oh, Pop!" she begged wearily. This was all so familiar, and stale. When John Franz started on this strain of self-accusation, she knew from long experience how the vein of it would run.

And when he turned suddenly and stumbled out of the room she called after him, knowing he would not heed; knowing all too well where he was going. . . .

The noonday sun was already steaming the moisture out of the earth, turning the valley roads again into ribbons of dust. Lynne Kingdom was not far from town, near the turn off for her father's ranch, when she saw a rider coming at an easy canter down the trail from the Saddle, his bronc's hoofs building tiny spurts of dust. She recognized the jughead before she could see its rider plainly, but she had quickly guessed who this was coming towards her. The knowledge put coldness into her dark eyes, and stiffness into her shapely body.

Wade Emery came nearer—as disreputable a figure as ever, she thought. A man of any pride would not let himself be seen like that, unshaven and in clothes that were next to rags. Even that unfortunate Doctor Franz made a better appearance. Perhaps, she thought, the two were in much the same boat; although she had to admit she had never noticed liquor on Wade Emery's breath.

As their horses neared, she saw that the man's eyes were on her face and it made her colour angrily. She tossed her black curls, under the chin-strapped, broad-brimmed hat, and her little chin was tilted high above her smooth, tanned throat and the turned-back collar of the riding-shirt, that only hinted of full, rounded breasts.

The man took his eyes away from her, passed her there on the road with head turned straight ahead and hand hard on the reins.

Wade Emery's thoughts were dark things as he rode on. Much better, he told himself bitterly, to be a nonentity as far as this girl was concerned—a mere range tramp below her noticing—than to have her hold the opinion his own stupidity and poor self-control had forced upon her. With such musings for poor company, he rode in past the shaded park, past the bandstand, up the hill to the town.

It might have been different, he told himself suddenly. The cards might have fallen otherwise. With a better shuffling before the deal, he could just as well have been an ordinary cowhand or even, for that matter, a rancher, with a reputation and a future as bright as any man's. He could have been one of the valley folk, who walked upon the streets of this town secure in the respect of themselves and of their neighbours.

He might even have dreamed of wandering through the park of a soft summer evening, the breeze and the stars around him, music from the bandstand floating through the trees and across the quiet night water. And Lynne Kingdom on his arm . . .

He made a grimace. He was forgetting Joel!

Steve Mallard was in doubt, and he looked it. Slouched low in his chair, spurred boot cocked up on the table edge beside a bottle and empty glass, he had a thumb hitched into shell belt and a cigar stuck between the fingers of the other hand. Through the blue smoke of that cigar, hanging in layers in the room's stale air, he studied the man in the other chair from under heavy brows; and the perpetual scowl was on the Bar M owner's sullen features. He said, gruffly: "What reason have I got to think I can trust you, Short?"

"Maybe none," Chuck Short agreed, and frowned. Ross Boyden was the man in the third chair. He leaned forward on his elbows, one hand making wet circles on the table with the bottom of his filled glass. His manner said that this was between Short and Mallard, and he would have nothing to add.

For a moment there was silence, except for the occasional noontime noises that drifted back from the main room of Phil Nolan's store. Mallard shrugged, then. "Well, if you're not on the level you're a bigger fool than I think. Supposing I take you at your word, then. What have you got to offer? What can you give me?"

"Plenty," said Short. "A line straight into the inside workings at Crown, for one thing."

"I already got that. Bart Yaeger."

"Him!" Short made an eloquent gesture. "He counts for less than nothing. But I'm old Kingdom's right-hand man."

Steve Mallard considered this. Ross Boyden said then: "Might be worth something, Steve. But we got that drifter to worry about first."

"What about him?" demanded Chuck Short, interest showing in his heavy-lidded eyes.

Mallard made a sour face, took a swallow from the whisky glass Boyden had refilled for him. He told briefly about the raid two nights ago, ending: "Ross let himself walk right into a trap. Got one man killed out of that stupid deal."

Ross Boyden's heavy face coloured, his craggy fist tightened on the glass. He swung his big head up; the look he gave Mallard was an angry one. "I tell you the guy ain't what he pretends! He's a hellion once he gets started!"

"Nonsense!" Coolly, the Bar M owner drained his glass. "The man's nothing but a dirty, unshaven saddletramp—you just blundered into his hands that night, is all. But I've got to get him off the Saddle before I can make another move. He's probably holding out for a price; and I'm damned if I'll knuckle down to a damned drifter that doesn't even pack a gun!"

Ross Boyden muttered grimly: "Maybe he don't pack one—but he goddam well knows what they're for. Me, I don't want to run head-on against him. Not a second time!"

"No?" Steve Mallard's lip twisted in heavy scorn. "You will if I tell you, bucko, or you'll draw your time! Because I got no place on my payroll for anyone yellow enough to be scared out by a thing like that!"

There was no answer. Chuck Short, embarrassed to witness such a scene, had got up and wandered to the dirt-streaked window. He turned away suddenly. "Speak of the devil! The drifter—he just rode in."

All at once Steve Mallard was on his feet, with a force of movement that also swept Ross Boyden out of his chair. "This is it!" exclaimed Mallard. "We'll take care of him right now! We'll see he don't get out of town alive!"

A quick look passed over Boyden's dark face. "You mean me, Steve?"

"Hell yes, I mean you. And there's Charlie Rook and one or two others—and that new man, Ivors; they're all at the Clover Leaf. Enough to do a job and do it final!"

He looked at Chuck Short, considering. "You better stay out of it," he said, at last. "You're still for Crown as far as anyone knows, and I don't want to take a chance of tipping our hand." He jerked his head at Boyden, then. "Come on, Ross! If we do it, we'll have to work fast!"

The foreman trailed him as he strode, quickly, from the room. Ross Boyden did not look too happy, of a sudden.

CHAPTER X

Wade Emery would not have ridden in this afternoon if it had not been for Joel Harris. It was two days now, and his friend would be lying in his bed, helpless, and hoping for some report. Though when he saw Lynne Kingdom riding away from town, Wade judged shrewdly that, likely, Joel already had his report; and he wondered, in that case, just what Lynne might have had to say about himself.

This was not pleasant speculation. He was scowling over it as his jughead took him down the dusty main street, past the courthouse and the two big saloons facing it. It was here that a man stepped suddenly from the shadow of a wooden awning and hailed him. "Gent in the bar across the street is talking about you, Emery. Says he knows you, wants to see you as soon as you hit town!"

Wade felt his face go hard, felt the leap of alarm inside him. So this was it! He had ridden hard and long to bury his trail, and now because of the too-prominent part he had let himself play in the crisis of Kingdom Range, the trail had been uncovered and the past had caught up with him.

He could cut and run again, of course, but that would be worse than futile. He couldn't hope to lose pursuit now that it had come this close on his heels. This was showdown—and it could not be evaded.

"Thanks," he said. Slowly, impassive face showing none of these thoughts, Wade reined in to a hitchrail and he stepped down there, and mechanically snubbed his reins about the chewed pole. His informant was watching, expression interested. When Wade Emery started across the muddy street, heading for the swinging doors of the Blue Chip, the man called after him: "No, not in there, pal. The other one."

Wade veered, changed direction and headed for the Clover Leaf. A few broncs were racked in front of it, all bearing the Bar M iron. Something said that this didn't fit in. But he went up the two wide steps, put his shoulder to a panel of the saloon's paint-peeling green doors, shoved through. Just inside he stopped, and then one slow glance at the interior of the dim, foul-smelling room made clear the inner warning he had felt.

And yet at the same time there came sharp relief. For none of the men he saw here was the law, or anyone from the past. Of the half-dozen watching him from along the bar, three at least were Bar M and the others, too, had the look of Steve Mallard's riders. There were Ross Boyden, Nate Ivors; another, shrivelled-up little gunslinger he had heard called by the

116

name of Charlie Rook. This whole set-up, then, was nothing but a Bar M deal. Even the barkeep, though nominally neutral, would remember that Bar M gave this saloon its principal business. Crown's friends usually, from consideration of policy, frequented the Blue Chip, which Thad Kingdom owned outright.

Wade Emery thought he did not have to be told what the purpose of this set-up was, or why a sentry had been posted to hail him and send him in here. Nothing to do now but play the hand as it lay. He said, mildly: "Someone here want to see me?"

His eyes singled out Ross Boyden as he said this, and it seemed to him as though Ross did not much like the look in them—as though the victim of this trap they had arranged showed that he understood too much what was going on. But Ross answered his question, bluntly. He said: "Yeah, I guess that's right." And added: "Take him, Charlie!"

It was Charlie Rook's signal. He came away from the bar, walking carefully and crouched a little, in typical gunfighter stance. His voice was edged with a thin, whining tone. "You filthy skunk, you murdered Jeff Bushong!" The man's right hand crept slowly down towards a jutting six-gun's handle. "Jeff was my bunkie. Two nights ago you shot him down, and you'll pay for it. Not packing an iron won't save you, either!"

Obviously the man was whipping himself into a killing rage—passion strong enough to let him shoot down an unarmed man. A swiftly sweeping glance showed Wade that the others were going to let him go ahead with it—then, in the shadows beyond Ross Boyden, he caught sudden sight of a face he had missed before, and it filled him with sharp interest. Bart Yaeger—a Crown rider—here with Steve Mallard's foreman . . .

All at once, with cool abruptness, Wade Emery turned his back full on the room and walked out of the Clover Leaf.

Behind him, as the swing doors beat the air together, he could hear Rook's voice rise into a scream of baffled hatred. "You dirty coward, come back here—" He did not pause. With quiet purpose Wade strode across the street again, straight for where he had tied his horse. But he did not mount. Instead, he opened a saddle-pocket, and brought out the things he had put there before coming down from Saddleback, on some unnamed prompting that he would need them: a six-gun, and a looped cartridge belt.

Quickly he slipped the belt around his waist, jerked the end through the buckle and thumbed the prong home. The holster, with the weight of the gun dragging it down, fell against his left hip with the weapon's wooden butt jutting forward. As it came there in its old, familiar place, the feel of it was a friendly and welcome thing to him. He was settling the belt into position when the voice of Dick Rudebaugh came suddenly from above him; he glanced up, quickly.

The sheriff stood on the courthouse veranda, watching intently with keen, blue eyes. "Gonna be some shooting, son?"

"Sheriff, this is a private matter!" Wade told him flatly. "Stay out of it."

"I aim to," Rudebaugh agreed. His tone held little emotion. Turning away from him Wade Emery headed back across the street with quick, firm strides. He was halfway to the Clover Leaf when Charlie Rook came slamming through its double doors, the other Bar M men at his back. Bart Yaeger, Emery noticed, was not among them.

Rook stopped short at sight of Emery, and the gun that Emery wore now. Behind him Ross Boyden and Ivors and the rest saw the gun, too; they took one look and then they scattered like quail, some diving back inside the saloon, the others leaping down to cover at either side of the long, warped steps.

Alone in the street, in full beat of the sun, Wade Emery stood and he called: "All right, Charlie Rook! If Bushong was one of those that raided Saddleback with you and Boyden night before last, then I reckon I killed him. I'm ready to settle it with you now!"

It had gone too far, and Rook could not back

out. He debated for only an instant, and then in impatient frenzy he made his try.

The gun seemed fairly to leap into the little man's fingers, with a speed that few enough could have hoped to equal. But good as he was, he really ought to have been better. For his gun was not the first to fire, and it was not his bullet that slammed home.

Those who watched had never seen anything like the lightning that moved the drifter's gun hand. It lashed across his waist, fingers curling about the forward-jutting gunbutt, and then with a flickering of the wrist the six-gun slipped out of holster, level and already aimed at Charlie Rook's thin middle. With the same motion that completed that cross-draw, the trigger worked; the hammer fell, and flame blossomed seconds before Charlie Rook's gun spoke.

In the mingling of shots Charlie Rook staggered, and then he broke and went down the steps to the board walk in a rolling sprawl. Burnt powder drifted and dissolved before Wade Emery's forward-bent, wide-legged shape. Through it he searched for further danger. He found it in a man that suddenly broke away from the frightened clutter of Bar M hands, and came legging towards Emery, calling his name.

It was Nate Ivors. Why he should thus forget his cynical philosophy of saving his own hide, and feel compelled to move out and pit himself against the speed of Wade Emery, he himself could not have told. Yet there he came, and Wade Emery slipped his gun back into holster and waited like that, arms dangling at full length, accepting the challenge. Ivors, coming on, waited tensely for the man to draw, determined not to be the first. Still, it was he who broke, and it was his hand that began the leap for gunmetal.

His speed was that of a professional, keyed high and with no flicker of wasted motion. The gun slid out of its greased, tied-down holster smoothly, came up fast and rocked into position. Then the lean fingers opened, loosely; the weapon slipped out of them and dropped into the dust at Ivors' feet. He looked down at it, dumbly, as though not understanding this or the gunroar beating into his ears. And then he fell lifeless in the mud, destroyed by his own pride of gunmanship.

Wade Emery swung his smoking weapon back towards the men who crouched in varied attitudes of astonishment and fear along the broad front of the Clover Leaf. There was no further challenge; and seeing this, he raised his voice and called.

"Bart Yaeger!" The name rang out across the stillness.

"You're the next, Yaeger! You lied about a good man, and then you gunned him down. I'm coming after you!"

He went forward, suddenly, at a run. He took the

steps at one leap, stabbed open the Clover Leaf's panels with his free hand, still-smoking gun held tight and ready in the other. Across the long room a door slammed, sharply. Without pausing, Wade went past staring men and wrenched that door open recklessly, went through.

Here was a corridor with a number of doors opening off into private gaming rooms. He wasted no time on them. At the end of the hall an outside door stood open in a white shimmer of sunlight, and Wade Emery's flat-heeled boots echoed hollowly as he headed for there. As he broke through into daylight, a movement to the side pulled him around fast—not fast enough.

Wade saw Yaeger's hunch-shouldered shape, the face white and scared. Then a gun bloomed in Yaeger's hand and Emery went into the mud, driven off his feet, pain skewering him hot and solid. He went clear around, fell heavily to hands and knees, and heard the scramble of Yaeger's boots as the man turned and fled.

The first nausea passed, and then Emery managed to get his feet under him again. He found the gun he had dropped and shoved it into holster, stood a moment there behind the Clover Leaf, considering. He would have to let Yaeger go, for now. That bullet streak along his ribs was bleeding freely and had to be attended to. Doc Franz was the man to see—and quickly.

None of the Bar M crowd had come after him,

but if they should he was in no shape to face them now. On this thought Wade Emery went away from that place, quickly, through the still heat of afternoon. He could hear the shouts that sounded from Main Street behind him, running out thinly on sun-warm air.

For long, a promise of violence had hung, like a cloud, over the town and range. Now two men lay dead, sprawled carelessly, their faces in the dust, and the violence had come. But Dick Rudebaugh was not thinking of that. He was not thinking of the Bar M hands who still spread across the front of the Clover Leaf and stared at their fallen comrades and each other, while the batwings still stirred a little from Emery's savage entrance. He was not even thinking of the single shot that had sounded somewhere out behind the saloon, the echoes of it rocketing across sun-blistered roofs.

He was remembering a thing that he had witnessed—the incredible speed with which a man's hand could sweep across his body and drag a six-shooter from leather. Emery had had the unprepossessing appearance of a saddletramp, and yet beneath it the man was a master with a gun. Rudebaugh, trying to square this fact with all his previous experience of the drifter, could not make it fit.

Then, from somewhere, came another memory. Something to do with that fabulous cross-draw.

He was sure he had seen it before, just once—up north it was! Dick Rudebaugh's heavy brows dragged down; he stared at nothing, trying to recall. There was a story that went with it—a story two, three years old. A grim and hideous story.

Then, he got it.

Out in the street now men were gathering, milling in a noisy impotency around the two sprawled bodies. A man called up to him: "Hey, Sheriff! This is in your province. Ain't you gonna do something about it?"

He shook himself. "Yeah," he answered, slowly. "One of you boys get the coroner. I'll be right with you!"

This thing he had stumbled upon had to be followed up, traced out while it was fresh in his mind. He turned and strode heavily into his office, to the desk with its messy muddle of papers and odds and ends. The sheriff's mind was as methodical as his belongings were untidy. Even on a scent as faint as this, he knew approximately where to look. He dropped into the swivel chair, leaned and forced open a drawer that was jammed full and that came out only with an effort. He pawed through this, and near the bottom found a stock of old reward dodgers, tied together with a woollen string. This he snapped with the jerk of one broad thumb, and began leafing through the stiff papers.

Near the middle was the one he wanted. The picture of Wade Emery, recognizable even without the beard stubble; a brief description; and the ugly story of a respected lawman abusing his office and his gunspeed, in order to rid himself of a personal enemy. Murder, the dodger called it. Dick Rudebaugh knew the reward had never been collected.

The sheriff sat for long seconds, staring at what he had found.

He had unearthed the secret of the Saddleback gunslick.

CHAPTER XI

Wade Emery came up to the rear of the doctor's house, where there was no gate at all in the fence, but only the socket where it should have hung. He went through this gap and to the kitchen door, where he waited what seemed like interminable minutes before anyone answered his knock.

It was Terry who swung the door wide, finally, and a startled look was in her eyes as she saw him and the blood staining the shirt above his ribs. "Come in!" she gasped. And as she quickly closed the door behind him: "Pop isn't here!"

He frowned. "I wonder if you'd get me some hot water, then? And antiseptic, and bandages, and maybe one of your dad's probes just in case I need it. I can patch myself, I guess."

He sat at the table, guarding his strength, as he waited for her to bring the things he needed. Then she was back with cloth, and scissors, and the rest, and he went to work.

The probe wasn't necessary. Bart Yaeger's lead had cut a clean furrow along his side, and antiseptic and a bandage was all it needed. By the time Emery had this done Terry came with a clean, threadworn white shirt. "One of Pop's," she told him. Wade didn't want to take it, but his own was a bloody ruin. As he drew it on carefully over the bulky shape of the bandage he said:

"I've got no money, Miss Franz. Maybe sometime I'll be able to repay you for your kindness!"

The tape was tight across his side. The gun, he found, did not drag too heavily. As he buckled it into place he saw that the girl was staring at him oddly; he did not know it was because the set of the gun seemed to change the whole shape and stand of his body, and that Terry Franz was thinking that here was a different man from the drifter she had seen in him before. He's taller, she thought. And straighter—

In the bedroom, Joel Harris stared as Wade entered and placed both brown hands on the round of the metal bedstead. Wade told him: "I just had a little brush with Steve Mallard's crowd. Had to kill a couple of them—Charlie Rook, and a new man."

"And they put a bullet in you!"

"Bart Yaeger did that. Looks like he's gone clear over to Mallard. He was in the Clover Leaf with the others."

The man in the bed stared. "Let's have that again!" he exclaimed.

Briefly, Wade Emery told his friend as much of the recent happenings as would be news to him. He said, in conclusion: "I've taken my gun out of wraps, and I'm wearing it from now on. Because things are coming to a head—Saddleback will be caught right in the middle!"

Joel Harris began, in despair: "I told you once what would come of mixing into my troubles! You went and almost got yourself killed. And now that this town has seen you in action, and has seen that greased-lightning cross-draw of yours—"

Wade Emery put up a hand thoughtfully, scraped it across the unsightly beard bristle that clouded his lean cheeks. He said slowly: "You're right at that!" And added with grim humour: "Thanks for reminding me—that there's no more need for this disguise!"

"Now, wait!" cried the other. But Emery had already turned towards the girl. "Your dad's razor, Miss Franz—I'd like to borrow it a few minutes if I can. . . ."

He shaved in Doc Franz's bedroom, with the doctor's long-shanked razor and hot water the girl brought for him. As the keen blade sheared through soap and bristle, wiping away the last remnant of Wade Emery's disguise, a deep and inward satisfaction filled him. He was a man of pride, and that pride had been sorely humbled before the scorn he had seen in the eyes of people like Dick Rudebaugh and Lynne Kingdom and the Franz girl. From looking like a saddletramp he had come very close to feeling like one; and now it was with a sense of removing some unclean stain from his body and his spirit that he put that shell away from him.

He towelled his face vigorously, and ran a comb through unruly brown hair and laid it smooth. He looked into the mirror, then. A new face peered back at him. Cheeks that tingled to the half-forgotten sting and pull of a blade showed paler than the sun-darkened forehead above them. It was a broad forehead, and a tapering face below it. The jaw showed as lean and slender, but with a stubborn squareness across the chin, and a touch of humour in the mouth. Not a handsome face, but one that held character; and Wade Emery looked at it with infinite satisfaction and ran a hand across the smoothness of the jaw.

Tiredness went through him then; the shock and loss of blood from that bullet had cost him more than he knew. He let himself down upon the edge of the doctor's bed, to rest a moment. He should get away from this house, he told himself; it would be a grave breach of trust if he should let his enemies trail him here and so involve the Franz family in trouble.

But when Terry Franz looked in, five minutes later, he was stretched out full length, arms thrown back above his head; and he was lost in deep and heavy sleep.

Sheriff Dick Rudebaugh went through the still heat of early afternoon to the telegraph office, where it was always shadowy and cool and the key's clicking made a pleasant busy music through the long summer days. The key was silent at the moment, the old telegrapher propped back in his chair asleep with the earphones strapped to his gleaming bald head. Without waking him, Rudebaugh moved ponderously to the counter and found a blank and stub of pencil. He hung his weight on one wide elbow and scowled at the paper, as he chewed the pencil and tried to think his message out. Composition never came easy for the sheriff, and now there was a good deal to be said and he had the county funds to remember.

Finally he went to work and after a great amount of deletion and interlineal changes had things the way he wanted them. The resulting message was still pretty lengthy, but it was as concise as Dick Rudebaugh knew how to make it; if his constituents wanted to fire him over a few extra words in a telegram, then let them. He was fairly well satisfied himself as he straightened up and dug for a handkerchief to swab the sweat of labour from his wide forehead. Then he decided he had better make a new copy so that the old man could be sure and read it.

The sheriff was just finishing this job when the key sprang to life and the telegrapher, waking, jumped his chair forward with a start and fell to work. He shut off the key, finally, and, removing the earphones, came forward with a greeting for his visitor. Rudebaugh nodded, shoved the scribbled paper across to him. "Send this off right away, will you, Joe? And how long do you reckon it will take for a reply?"

The old man's quick eyes scanned the message, and his brows rose with interest. But he said only: "Montana, huh? Well, it's entirely up to the sheriff's office at the other end, how long it will take. What shape their files are in, and how interested they are—you know as much about that as I would."

"All right," grunted Dick Rudebaugh. "When the answer comes, send it right over to me, will you? To the house if it should get here after office hours."

"Sure." The old man added: "I'll shoot this right off. Who's paying for it—the county?"

"Did you think I was?" countered the sheriff. He waited a little longer, while the telegrapher went back to his chair and his earphones, and he listened to the first experimental tappings of the key. Then the sheriff wheeled and strode out again into the sultry day.

He knew the old man could be trusted to keep his mouth shut about the contents of that telegram, and yet for some reason Dick Rudebaugh was vaguely uneasy as he trudged back, beneath the dusty trees, to his office in the courthouse. There were reasons why he would not want the truth about Wade Emery to leak out before he received the answer to his wire. He understood that nagging uneasiness, therefore, when he walked into his office and found that he had left the reward dodger lying in plain sight atop his desk. Rudebaugh frowned, and for some reason turned for a sharp look across his shoulder. The room was empty, of course, but the door to the dark hall had stood wide open all the while he was gone. Moreover there was his deputy; Lee Ball had a tongue that was greased too slick for anyone's good. A gossipmonger—that was Lee, even when his attentions were well-meaning. Dick Rudebaugh slumped into his swivel chair, and scowled darkly at the floor.

He hardly knew why, but an uneasy inner prompting said that he had blundered badly. Perhaps no one had seen that dodger; yet he heartily wished he had taken greater precautions with it.

If the news about Wade Emery spread too fast and too soon, it could only complicate the already muddled and dangerous affairs of this mountain valley range. . . .

Bart Yaeger found Steve Mallard in the back room at Nolan's; Chuck Short was there too. Yaeger slipped in and slammed the door and put his back to it, and he had a wild look about him that was something like that of a trapped animal.

Steve, hitching his chair about for a look at him, made a wry face. "I thought maybe you were still running!" He jerked a thumb at the bottle and glasses on the table. "You better give yourself a drink."

"Thanks!" Yaeger took his hump-shouldered form away from the door, sidled over and poured the liquor with hands that still shook. He downed it in a quick toss of the whisky down his throat. "That devil!" He added a foul string of epithets that relieved some of his injured pride and his fear. "You saw what he did to Rook and Ivors—gunplay like I never saw before or even heard about. And then to have him start out after me—!"

Steve Mallard said, irritation edging his voice: "The trap we laid went awful bad on us. Two men killed—two good men! Maybe I been too rough on Ross Boyden, after all, for the fluke he pulled the other night at Saddleback; because whatever this Wade Emery looks like, he's certainly a gunmaster!"

He shot a sharp glance at Yaeger. "The hell of it is, Bart, you went and let yourself be seen in the Clover Leaf, and that told Emery something. He's probably guessed the connection between you and me, and that you told a few fibs about that stick-up. Certainly it's the reason he went after you when he'd laid out Charlie and Nate. It means he's the one most dangerous man we've got to cope with—even more dangerous than Dick Rudebaugh!"

"What are we going to do about him?" Chuck

Short demanded. "He's dropped out of sight since the shooting. His bronc's still standing at the hitchpole where it was tied, so he must be in town somewhere. But you won't get anyone to stand up to his gun now! A bullet in the alley is the only way we can hope to get rid of him."

Bart Yaeger said, bitterly: "I dunno about that, even. I shot him. It didn't stop the devil!"

"You did what?" Steve Mallard straightened sharply.

"Shot him—sure! I laid for him out back of the Clover Leaf, and put a bullet in him the minute he showed. It knocked him off his feet—threw him clear around. But he got up again, and I—reckon the sight of it rattled me. I beat it, and laid low in the Blue Chip until I got my nerve back!"

Chuck Short slapped a hand against the table top, so hard that bottle and glasses danced. "God damn it!" he growled. "You had him right then! One more slug would have finished him—if you hadn't been too yella to—"

"Shut up!" Steve Mallard cut him off. The heavy black brow was a line that dragged down upon his crooked nose; his full, sullen lips were tight. "That tells us one thing, anyhow. We know where Emery is."

"Where?" demanded Yaeger.

"Why, at the doc's, of course! His pal Harris is there, and it's the only place the man could go to have a bullet wound taken care of. Ten to one Wade Emery is there at this very moment."

Short grunted: "Well, put men around the place, then. Tag him whenever he steps outside."

The other nodded a little, reluctantly. "That may have to be it! But it's damned slow. He might get wind and stay inside. And there's Rudebaugh— the sheriff could give us a lot of trouble if he found out about a thing like—"

The door was jerked open and big Ross Boyden strode in; and the look of his heavy face said that the man was terrifically worked-up. With the eyes of the three on him he came forward, put his heavy hands flat upon the table top and dropped his weight upon them. Leaning forward like that, his eyes filled with keen excitement, he looked around at them all. "News, Steve!" he exclaimed. "You know that deputy of Rudebaugh's?"

"Ball? What about him?"

"He was just over at the Clover Leaf, getting a drink—and talking his head off! He's seen an old reward dodger Rudebaugh dug up somewhere. This Emery jigger—he's a renegade lawman from someplace in Montana, wanted there for murder. The word is all over town by now!"

"Good lord!" exclaimed Chuck Short. "So that's what it is! I knew there was something in back of Emery!"

Keen speculation showed the rapid working of Steve Mallard's crafty brain. Suddenly he turned on the Crown foreman. "Are there any more of your men in town this afternoon?"

Short said: "I don't know." He in turn looked at Yaeger, who nodded. "Two or three are in the Blue Chip, I think."

"Get them!" Steve ordered, speaking to Short. "Take them over to the doc's, and finish Emery! We know he's there—and he's hurt already, and he shouldn't give too much of a fight. You've got every excuse. The man's a wanted criminal; his boss has stolen from Kingdom. It'll look better if Crown takes the initiative—less like it might be a follow-up of that fiasco this afternoon."

Short said, frowning: "You want this thing done now?"

"Of course—the sooner the better—before Rudebaugh may be forced to take a hand. And," he added, "if the sheriff tries to interfere don't take anything off him. You've got the appearance of legality behind you and this is our chance to be rid of the last danger from Saddleback. Then the way will be open for us to go ahead."

"All right."

Short got his hat from the table and dragged its floppy brim down low over his receding hairline, and his eyes were grim and maybe even a little frightened. But he had an assignment and he told Bart Yaeger, shortly: "Let's go, Bart. We'll stop at the Blue Chip first—"

They went out of there in a quick roll of boot-heels and ringing scrape of spurs.

When Terry's fingers touched his arm, Wade Emery came awake all at once, as a cat does, and rolled lightly off the bed to his feet. She had one warning finger against her lips; she said: "There are men coming along the street. I think they're headed here!"

Instantly he had gone past her and to the front of the house, and a glance around the edge of the frayed curtain at the big window by the door showed him all he needed to know. Even now the half-dozen Crown men were turning in before the doctor's house; Chuck Short in the lead tried the broken gate and then in impatience kicked it aside, hurling it clear off the remaining hinge. The men came on, tramping solidly up the walk to the porch.

Wade turned to the girl. "It's Crown," he said. "I thought at first it was someone who wanted me!"

"You mean—?" She indicated the half-closed door of Joel Harris's room, alarm leaping in her face. Wade nodded.

"Looks as though that's what they've come for!" As the first sound of boots struck the sagging porch, he added quickly: "You answer the door. I'll duck into the bedroom and if they're looking for trouble—they'll find it!"

"Wait!" she cried; but Chuck Short's heavy fist was already mauling the door panels and the Crown foreman's voice was yelling: "Open up here!" Without any other word Emery whirled sharply and went through into the bedroom.

Here Joel Harris was waiting, bolt upright in bed, an unspoken question on his lips. Wade silenced him with a gesture. Gun in hand now, he had the door closed almost to a crack and he pressed against it, listening, as the sound came of the big front door's opening. Terry Franz's first stammered question was lost in Short's bellow: "You got a criminal hiding in your house, and we want him! He murdered two men here today and he's wanted for another killing in Montana—"

The man behind the door heard this in a rush of consternation. The secret, then, was out. And, contrary to his guess, the Crown men were here, not for Joel, but for himself!

He knew by his friend's look that Joel Harris too had heard, and understood. Out in the other room, Terry Franz was saying: "I have no idea what you're talking about!"

"Don't give me that!" Chuck Short growled at her. "We know he came here, and we mean to have him. Stand aside!" A brief scuffle of feet told how he thrust the door wide, shoving Terry Franz to one side, and came on into the house with his men trooping after him.

The one window of the room stood open.

Seeing only one course before him, Wade Emery went to this window quickly, pushed curtains out of the way and threw a leg across the sill. "Don't let them know I was here," he gave Joel Harris final warning. "It would only mean trouble for the doc's family!" Then he was gone, the curtains swaying behind him.

Hugging the wall he ran swiftly along the side of the house, away from the front. The beat of the sun was a heavy weight across the still afternoon. Then as he reached the back and took the corner the boom of a six-gun met him.

He was not expecting this and it hauled him up sharp. The bullet slapped into clapboards not a yard from him. Then Wade saw the man, over at the gap in the fence—posted there, of course, on the chance Wade Emery should make a break for it!

Emery's own weapon was coming up for a shot. The other man got a second bullet off just before Wade could fire, but perhaps he was rattled at actually crossing sights with the gun-master who had downed Charlie Rook and Nate Ivors. At any rate he missed wildly, and then Emery's shot came over and the man buckled and spilled back against the picket fence, hit the earth and lay there stirring and moaning.

Wade Emery had time to be glad he hadn't killed the man; but he knew the noise of the shots would bring Chuck Short and he could not loiter.

He sprinted across the bare yard, through the fence. Shouts, running feet were echoing through the doctor's house as he turned and fled along the alley. Cinders ground and spurted underfoot. Just as he neared the alley's end, a gun spoke behind him, and, glancing back, he saw that men were pouring after him out of the doctor's back lot.

Then he caught sight of a saddled horse, tied, with drooping head, under a big cottonwood in a neighbouring yard. He had never stolen another man's bronc, but it looked like this would have to be the first time. In saddle, perhaps he could hang on and somehow get away; but afoot it would be a matter of quick capture and perhaps good men getting hurt. He could not have that.

No one challenged him as he reached the tied horse, jerked loose the reins that held it to the cottonwood bole. It was a dappled grey, that looked to have no particular speed or endurance. But its four legs were better than his two.

He was just trying for the stirrup as three of the running Crown men showed along the alley.

CHAPTER XII

An exchange of shots behind the Franz house was Chuck Short's first warning that Emery was getting away from him. He half-saw the expression of dismay that flooded Terry's white face; then he had shoved her to one side and went clumping through the rear door, his men at his heels. Out back, the man Short had posted there lay twisting and moaning against the fence, Wade Emery's bullet in him.

This sight gave Short a sudden access of caution; he was all at once in no hurry to face Wade Emery, after this proof that Emery was not too badly hurt to give a good accounting of himself across gunsights. So the Crown foreman turned instead to his men and cried: "Yaeger! Down the alley—don't let him escape!" And then he turned back to confront the pale and frightened girl.

"I suppose you're gonna tell the law you didn't know what kind of a criminal you were hiding out here!" he bellowed.

Terry Franz retorted: "No, I didn't! And I don't see any star on your chest. Get out!"

His face coloured. "I'll take no talk from a drunken doctor's brat—"

"Short!" That voice thundered through the tiny

143

house. "Stop brow-beating the girl, you hear me?"

Lantern-jawed face gone hard, Chuck Short shoved open the door of the bedroom and tramped inside for a look at Joel Harris. What he was about to say died on his lips; for his eye, happening to drop to the floor, suddenly widened. He came forward, stooped, straightened with a length of braided leather in his hands. A riding-crop. Lynne Kingdom's!

Short had felt this whip laid across his cheek, one time. Something of the fury and the sting of that occasion came back to him now and whipped keen rage through him. He pinned the hurt man with a narrow stare. "Was Miss Kingdom here to see you? Answer me!"

Joel Harris made no answer. Sudden jealousy tightened Short's hand over the whip and he whirled on the two Crown men who had stayed behind and were watching from the doorway. "Take him!" the foreman cried. He flung a pointing hand towards the bed. "We've had enough foolishness with this man. We'll put him in jail—now—where he belongs!"

One of the Crown men hesitated. He said: "We got no authority to move this man, Chuck."

"Franz and his whole household are discredited by hiding that Wade Emery killer! If Thad knew his daughter had been here he'd insist on Harris being moved, and the sheriff himself wouldn't dare object. So, take a hold and get him out!"

Crowded from the room, Terry Franz watched in horror as the two Crown men went in to obey their foreman's command. She couldn't see much—only the big bodies of the men going forward, and then a tussle at the bed. After that they had Joel Harris dragged out and onto his feet, and she heard his groan as the bullet-smashed knee buckled under his weight. Terry sobbed, hands pressing her ears. She had to stop them—

Suddenly she whirled away, ran and flung open the back door. "Jim!" she cried frantically, over and over. The echoes of her own voice mocked her. Jim, she had thought, could go for their father or the sheriff. But the boy had disappeared somewhere.

With quick decision Terry went out into the sunlight, and she started to run. The wooden cupola of the courthouse, with its circling pigeons, showed ahead through trees and across rooftops, and she sighted on that. She ignored staring eyes, kept on without pausing until she had reached the steps of the big building and went up them two at a time. Then she was in the dark hallway, and the door of the sheriff's office was standing open. When she reached this, she had to catch at the doorpost, her panting body sagging against it. For a moment she could not get breath to speak.

Dick Rudebaugh was not there. The deputy, Lee

Ball, sprawled in the sheriff's swivel chair, one spur hooked on the edge of the littered desk; he looked up in quick surprise as the girl appeared in the doorway—and went on looking.

In running, she had lost the handkerchief from about her hair, and it fell to her shoulders now in a yellow cloud. Running had put colour into the pale cheeks, also, and the swell of her breasts lifting and falling beneath the threadbare gingham dress caught the man's eye. Suddenly he took his boot down from the desk, a new interest showing in him. All the times he had seen Terry Franz around town, he had never realized before she had anything worth a second glance.

"Where—where is he?"

"Dick?" Lee Ball shrugged. "I dunno." He came to his feet, slouched towards her with a grin building across his face. "Maybe there's something I can do for you, huh?"

Her mouth twisted a little. "I don't reckon so." Terry didn't think much of Lee Ball. Suddenly she had dashed away again, leaving him to stare after her stupidly, and running as if she was heading across the street towards the Blue Chip.

She had never entered a saloon in her life, but she knew her father was here and she did not hesitate. A breath of stale beer and sweat gusted out across the swinging doors; she pushed through and halted a moment just inside, timidly.

At the bar men were gaping, grinning, and one made a remark just loud enough for her to hear. Terry had no time to be frightened or insulted. She had caught sight of her father, all alone at a table towards the rear of the dimly-lighted room. She went to him at once.

William Franz did not even look up. He slouched loosely in his chair, his tie disordered, lean doctor's hands spread limp across the green baize. A bottle stood before him, and a filled glass that held an amber jewel of light in its liquid depths. He stared at this with weak blue eyes transfixed.

"Pop!" cried Terry. He did not move. Frantic, she seized the thin arm in both hands, shook him. "You gotta come, Pop! They'll kill Joel if you don't stop them—"

With a slow, sideward tilting, her father slid off the chair and heavily against her. She could not hold up his unconscious body, and had to let him slide to the floor. From the bar behind her a coarse guffaw sounded. She whirled on the men, furious tears smarting her eyes. "You could at least help me!" she cried.

A bartender came around the end of the mahogany then, moved over and got his arms under the drunken man and hoisted him back into the chair, where William Franz's head dropped forward upsetting the bottle. The bartender caught him, leaned him back against the chair and the head lolled limply, eyes glassy, mouth sagging open.

"I'm damn' sorry, Miss Franz," said the aproned man, and his voice was not lacking in sympathy. "I can't keep him out of here, and Thad Kingdom won't let me refuse to sell him liquor. Says the doc's money is as good as anybody else's and if I don't take it I'll get canned."

"All right, Buck," she answered dully. "I guess you can't help it, if that's old Kingdom's orders." She started to turn away, but the man stopped her.

"Here," he said, and dragged a wallet from the drunken man's pocket. "Maybe you better take this, ma'am, before somebody else does. I can't always keep my eye on these guys."

"Thanks, Buck." She took the wallet. It was flat enough already. She carried it clutched in both hands as she went out of the saloon.

She reached the steps just as Chuck Short and the two Crown men were coming along the street, and they had Joel Harris with them. They were dragging him, his heels scraping the planks of the walk; his head bobbed, unconscious, and the face looked bloodless and dead. Terry tried to move forward, but her strength failed her and she went limp and sagged against a wooden roof support, tears half-blinding her.

Through their shining film she watched the Crown men get Joel Harris up to the veranda of the courthouse and in across the sill.

The cells were on the second floor, with a heavy, iron-bound door opening on a landing in the dark and narrow stairs. When Chuck Short demanded the key to this door, Lee Ball put up a squawk at first.

"I can't do that!" the deputy exclaimed. "You got no authority. You got no right to ask me!"

"You like your job, don't you?" growled Short. "Then come across—or Thad Kingdom will have that star jerked right off your shirt front!"

"Oh, these are Kingdom's orders?" And at Short's nod he backed down and fetched the key ring from Rudebaugh's desk. "I can't actually give you the keys—Dick wouldn't like it. But I'll go along and you show me what you want done."

"I just want you to open up a cell while we shove a crook inside of it."

Lee Ball hardly glanced at the limp shape of the prisoner. He led the way down the gloomy hall to where narrow stairs angled upwards, back towards the building's rear door. They creaked and sagged a little under the weight of so many men, and Joel's boots bumped against the treads as he was dragged up them. Under the deputy's key, the heavy iron door swung open on another corridor lined with cells.

Here it was stifling, sweltering, for air didn't seem to circulate through this big room; though there was much sunlight from the unshaded windows, to lay their dazzling, bar-striped patterns across the splintered wooden floor. All the cells were empty at the moment, and into the first of them Short's men hauled Joel Harris and piled him, unceremoniously, onto the bunk with its thin mattress.

The Crown foreman stood for a long minute scowling down at the unconscious man. Short had Lynne Kingdom's riding-crop in his hand; his fingers tightened around it and for a moment he knew an impulse to raise the whip and strike Harris across the face with it. But with these others watching, he refrained. Instead, he let a sneer touch his mouth as he muttered: "Maybe your lady friends won't come calling on you, here!" Then he pulled at the leather-sewed brim of his shapeless hat and, turning, strode out of the cell and let Lee Ball clang the door shut and lock it.

Tramping down the narrow stairs he could hear the deputy saying: "Dick Rudebaugh ain't gonna like this, God damn it!" Chuck Short was not in a mood to give that any thought.

At Nolan's store, there was no one in the back room to greet him but Bart Yaeger. Short scowled at sight of him. "I thought I sent you and the boys to get Emery!"

"He found a bronc and got away from us. Bib and Shorty went after him. I thought I'd better let you know what happened."

"Oh." Chuck Short frowned, not liking this. "Where's Steve?"

"Gone when I got here. Nolan gave me a message from him, for you."

He handed over a fold of paper. Short thumbed it open and glanced quickly at Steve Mallard's heavy, solid scrawl. For a moment the meaning of what he read hardly sank in, and when it did the audacity of it struck him like a blow that nearly staggered him. He looked up slowly. "You read this?" And at Yaeger's nod: "You think you can handle your part?"

"I don't know why the hell not!"

"Okay." The Crown foreman read the words a second time, and shrugged. "Well, that's it, then." He stuffed the paper into a pocket of his jeans. "You'll be staying here in town. But I got to be hitting the trail; because the day is wearing thin!"

Sunset was, indeed, not far away when he rode into Crown headquarters. Short, with Mallard's note in his pocket as a reminder that he had a busy night ahead of him, told a hand to take care of his bronc and himself headed for the one-room shack that went with the foreman's job. He was a poor housekeeper, and things accumulated. He got a bottle and glass from the shelf and tossed off a drink to wash the dust down his throat. Then he located a new box of shells in the chest of drawers, and an oily rag, and took these to a broad-armed chair beside the window.

Here he unhooked his gunbelt, and drawing the six-shooter from its holster set to work cleaning and oiling it, as he hummed a nameless tune, idly, between his teeth. Then he examined the loads, punched out one that looked defective and replaced it with a gleaming new cartridge from the box that he broke open.

Satisfied with the gun, he took up the belt and began stuffing shells, thick with grease, into the canvas loops. Once, in the process of this, he happened to glance up and through the window and caught sight of Thad Kingdom and his daughter walking together on the lawn beside the big house.

Chuck Short paused in his work, studying the slim shape of the girl, and the way the faint hint of a sunset breeze across the knoll lifted her hair in a dark cloud and touched the hem of her riding skirt. He felt again an echo of desire for her, scowled over it. Then he turned and his eyes lit on the little riding-crop which he had flung down upon the table, and that and the memories it evoked curdled his feelings into something with a very sour taste.

Suddenly he was on his feet, buckling the gun where it belonged, and he took the riding-crop and went out with it, straight across the yard to the house. Lynne and her father had disappeared around towards the front of the building; Short strode firmly after them, and then when he

152

had them in sight again eased his pace and, as they turned and saw him coming, sauntered up slapping at his boot top with the quirt.

Both saw it, of course; and recognition of her quirt widened Lynne's eyes and put alarm into her face. This gave Short a satisfaction that he didn't let show in his heavy-lidded eyes. He came straight towards father and daughter, nodding and touching the leather-sewed hat-brim in greeting. He said, respectfully and smoothly: "This is yours, I believe, Miss Kingdom. I guess you must have left it."

She looked at the little braided whip, and her face was blanched. She put out a slim hand and accepted the quirt, and her voice was shaky. "I— suppose I did," she agreed. "Thank you, Chuck." She managed a smile, but it stopped at her mouth and never reached her eyes.

"I thought you'd be missing it," he went on, blandly. "I picked it up off the floor, in the doctor's house in town." He touched his hat-brim again, would have turned away but the thunderous voice of old Thad Kingdom stopped him.

"You did *what?*"

His answer came, not from Chuck Short, but from Lynne herself. Something in his voice and the furious look of him had roused her own inherent stubbornness. She told him: "He found it at the Franz house—where I went to see Joel

Harris after learning, roundabout, how you'd had him shot and thrown under arrest on some trumped-up charge!"

Fury straightened old Thad to his full, lean height; his eyes beneath their blue-veined lids turned upon his daughter in a look compounded of anger and disbelief. "Are you accusing me of a lie—you, my own daughter? And would you actually make a fool of yourself by going to see that jailbird?"

"Someone's lying," she countered, stoutly. "I don't insist that it's you. But I'll see Joel wherever and whenever I please!"

"Why, you must be—" For once old Thad was speechless, his mouth dropping open on words that refused to come. He ducked his chin into the turkey wattles of his neck, and stared with fierce amazement at the spirit of this girl. For her part, Lynne's cheeks were ablaze with angry colour, her trim shape taut with indignation. Chuck Short, standing by, had his thumbs hooked into belt and a crooked grin on his lantern-jawed face, thoroughly enjoying this scene he had staged and started unfolding.

His pleasure ended abruptly. For suddenly Lynne cast a furious glance in his direction and she exclaimed: "If you want to argue this, Dad, it's all right with me—but let's not do it here in front of the help!"

That wiped the grin from Chuck Short's mouth,

quick enough. It straightened him like a slap in the face—or a cut from Lynne's sturdy little riding-crop. His jaw tightened. He said: "I beg your pardon!" in an icy tone that held no hint of begging in it. And then he turned and walked away from there, and neither the old man nor the girl seemed to notice that he had gone.

But in Chuck Short cold fury was a pulsing thing that throbbed now, with an intensity that hurt. He strode to his cabin, walked inside and slammed the door hard and stood with fists clenched, staring blackly at nothing. Sunset colours came through the window, staining the walls with their redness; but Short hardly noticed.

He was filled with a burning impatience, suddenly, for night to come—for the time when the pride of old Kingdom, and of his stiff-necked, self-willed daughter, should be broken finally and humbled in the dust!

CHAPTER XIII

It was touch and go with Wade Emery. Where those two Crown hands had found horses so quickly he had no idea, but they found them and they also had picked up three other riders somewhere, and they had located Emery's trail outside of town and were hounding him through the long afternoon. The sun was merciless on the valley's lower slopes. Moreover the dappled grey gelding he appropriated possessed a jolting sort of gait that stirred up all the weakness in Emery's bullet-slashed body. He found himself hanging on grimly, trying every trick he knew to lose his pursuers without avail, and being driven further into the lower hills, and directly opposite to the way he wanted to go.

After a half-hour of this his mount was tiring and the rider felt himself rapidly playing out. The chase could not go on forever. When he saw this clearly, Wade Emery suddenly drew rein and twisted about in saddle for a look at the back trail.

He sat in the sun-flecked shadow of cotton-woods that grew on the slope of a ridge, flanking a stony-throated gully. Beyond lay an open glade, washed with sunlight that shimmered a little before his aching eyes. His pursuers would be taking that open stretch in another minute, hot on the trail. And it was here he would have to make his stand; because further flight was out of the question.

Shooting from saddle was poor business. Emery slung a leg across the withers of his bronc and slid to the ground. A rifle was in the boot and he dragged it out; it seemed strangely heavy to him. He jacked it open, saw the coppery gleam of cartridges in the breech. Satisfied, he snapped it shut again.

All at once his legs felt rubbery beneath him. He had not guessed how badly the jolting and the bullet would have sapped his strength. He let the rifle stock down against the earth and dropped an arm across the grey's back, rested that way a moment trying to gather his resources. The bronc's sweaty hide steamed; it shifted iron-shod hoofs in the rubble of the hillside, blowing, and fell still. For a moment there was only the faint breath of the breeze in tree heads, throwing their shifting shadows across the slope.

Yonder, five horsemen came sweeping over the sunbright crest, against the sky's blue, and came tearing down towards the gully with a rush and a clatter. Wade Emery tried to haul his rifle up and rest its barrel across the saddle, but the effort was too much and he took a sudden swoop into nothingness. His fingers found the horn and he clutched it and hung on that way, his weight dragging the tree sidewards as he sagged at the knees, face pressed against the hot, smooth leather of the kak. With all the need for action, he could not move or even think clearly, through the black gauzy veil that dropped alarmingly across his brain and seemed to wrap him round.

After what seemed like a long time the veil lifted somewhat and stiffness came into his legs, and at once he remembered and got the rifle up into position. He stared then, dully, not comprehending. The five who came after him had vanished. Before him the sun-smitten hill, and the gully at its foot, lay empty and silent.

Then he understood. Somehow they had missed him, there in the dappled shadow of the cottonwood growth. They had hammered straight past and up into the throat of the gully, and for the moment—for how long?—his trail was clear.

He wished he knew what amount of time had elapsed while he clung to the saddle, half-conscious. Before too long, the pursuers would realize that they had slipped up somewhere, and would be coming back. This moment of good fortune could give him at most only a breathing space, which would soon be gone if he failed to take full advantage of it.

So, dragging himself once more into the saddle, he swung his weary mount around and gave it the steel. The grey grunted in protest. Wade Emery put it to the steep slope of the hill and it went up slowly through the cottonwood grove, head bobbing, shoes digging into the earth. Beyond this ridge was the gentle, easy sweep of a long hogback, and farther on Wade could see the burnished gleam of the river, with reeds swaying in backwash near the shore. Long grass swept the stirrup leathers as the grey took him down towards the dazzle of sun-smear on flowing water. Wind ran through the grass in waves of light and dark. And there was silence except for the call of a meadowlark hidden somewhere out there. . . .

Smoky shadows of evening were hovering when Lynne Kingdom led her pinto out of its special stall in the Crown barn, and cinched on the light, tooled saddle. The rig had cost old Thad Kingdom a lot of money; there was even a boot to hold a small carbine, and Lynne had this gun with her and she shoved it into leather. Night was coming on, and she was riding, and she didn't know how long she would be gone—or, for that matter, exactly where she was headed. Likely she would end up at the next ranch, the Lazy F, and stay for supper with her girlfriend, Jessie Ferguson. She'd told no one she was going, and no doubt old Thad Kingdom would worry about her when he heard. Lynne didn't care much. She was plain mad over that business about the quirt. And she didn't want to talk to anyone on Crown, right now.

She was about to swing into saddle when she

saw the rider on the tired grey, coming across swells at the rear of the ranch buildings. Something about his appearance made her hesitate, frowning a little. She took her boot toe out of stirrup and stood by the pinto's side, waiting as he neared.

From a distance the shape of the man seemed familiar; when he got closer and she could see his face, Lynne was not so sure. Then she realized that it was indeed Wade Emery, but that he had removed the beard stubble that formerly clouded his face. Clean-shaven, her guess about him was confirmed; this man had a strength in him. He was not one who would, by nature, choose the easy trail of the saddletramp.

But remembering the unpleasant incident between the two of them that morning, upon the Saddle, she held a reserve as he came up to her, touching a finger to shapeless hat-brim. She said, her voice edged with wariness: "Were you looking for someone?" She had noticed how his pale blue eyes had been at work, prying into the shadows piled beyond the barn's wide doors, searching the deserted ranch yard.

"Yes, I was. Bart Yaeger . . ."

The name, and the tone in which it was spoken, startled her. She found herself saying, quickly: "What do you want with him?"

"To kill him, I suppose. If I can't beat the truth out of him!"

Something made her move forward, place one hand on the neck of his bronc and tilt her dark head to stare at this strange man. The horse, she could tell, had been ridden hard; the neck was wet with sweat and the skin twitched under her hand. She said, breathlessly: "What is it you're thinking, Wade Emery? That Bart lied—about the trouble with the payroll?"

"Yes, I've got everything but proof."

For a moment she could not answer, while the shadows thickened about them. Finally she said: "I hope—for Joel's sake—that you can get that proof! Otherwise, I'll always feel somehow guilty; because Crown did this to Joel—and I am part of Crown!"

Wade Emery considered her silently. Suddenly he asked her: "Are you in love with Joel Harris?" But then, without waiting for an answer, he added sombrely: "I had no right to ask that! Please forget that I did. I—don't seem to know how to talk to a person like you, Miss Kingdom. You saw that once before, today, I'm afraid . . . As for Bart Yaeger, Crown has no responsibility for what he did. He was acting under orders from Steve Mallard. The man has sold out his loyalty to Bar M."

"How horrible!" she exclaimed. She frowned thoughtfully. "I'm sure he hasn't been around at all this afternoon."

"I reckon I know where to find him, then."

"Where?"

"Across the Saddle—with Mallard."

He was about to turn his bronc away when Lynne halted him with a little cry, the truth striking her forcibly. "You've been hurt! I'm sorry—I didn't realize—"

"It doesn't matter," he said, briefly. And yet he hesitated, and something made him blurt out: "You'll be hearing the whole story about me soon, Miss Kingdom—or at least one version. You'll find it's not a very pretty story. I want to ask you—please!—to keep an open mind; because, like most things, this has another side to it." Lynne said nothing. Perhaps he misread her silence, for he added roughly: "It's not what you think of me that matters. But Joel Harris is my friend, and if you believe what they say about Wade Emery it can't help but affect the stand of things between the two of you.

"Joel can tell you the whole facts of the case. Ask him—and please believe what he says!"

And, cutting off any reply the girl might have made, he sent his mount forward with a sudden spurt of speed. He was gone at once, the growing dark swallowing him up. For long minutes Lynne Kingdom stood listening to the fading hoofbeats, thinking of that strange conversation. Her frown was a troubled one.

Wade Emery pushed on, up the increasing lift of the hills to the gap of the Saddle. Full dark settled rapidly as he climbed. He could hear the wheeze of his horse's wind, feel a tired stumble, and knew the grey was very near to played out. He knew now he should have tried for a change of mounts back there at Crown. He tried resting his bronc at frequent intervals, as it took him up the skirt of the pass; to do this he climbed from saddle, once or twice slipped the bit to let the weary animal have a pull at the scant grass or muzzle a drink from a cold mountain spring.

The very effort of mounting and dismounting— doing this ever more frequently, as the grey's stamina began to run out—suddenly told on the rider. As he reached the top of the last steep grade, and moved once more to hitch a leg across saddle and swing down, Wade Emery knew an alarming seizure of dizziness and pain that ran through him and left him limp, so that he had to clamp one hand upon the saddlehorn to keep him in his place, while the weary animal shifted its body against this new distribution of weight.

He knew all at once that he made demands upon his body that were too great, and that the bullet streak in his side was beginning to tell. He couldn't keep on like this. Certainly, neither he nor the grey was in any shape to continue the ride to Bar M. So, instead, when strength returned, he reined aside from the trail and headed his bronc towards Saddleback.

Cold night wind, touched by the snows of

Baldy's cap, sang overhead, rattled dry brush that clung to the rock. The little spread was deserted and dark when he came in on it—just as it had been left that morning. He stepped down a little shakily, slipped off the bridle, loosened the cinch strap, dragged the saddle from the grey's back. The tree seemed terribly heavy all of a sudden; its weight pulled Emery forward and he let it thud to the ground. The grey shied away at that and then wandered off, tiredly, to look for something to eat.

Wade Emery went towards the cabin, half-dragging the saddle, and leaving it by the door, went up the two steps and into the dark room. He felt his way to the bunk, let himself down upon it. In the dark he lay there and again was alarmed at the weakness that was in him.

He fumbled for the bandage over his wound, found that there had been no seepage of blood. Relieved with this, he next thought of food. Black, strong coffee; or perhaps even a drag at a whisky bottle, to give him its bracing strength. He thought there was a pint in the packing case cupboard beside the stove. He lifted his legs over the edge of the bunk, and got a little unsteadily to his feet.

He was like that when horsemen came swooping into the yard outside, with a clatter of hoofs and jingle of bit chains.

Standing there, Emery thought quickly. There

was no reason at all to think these visitors were friendly; and if they were enemies, there were far too many for him to face in his present uncertain state. One hand had dropped to the forward-jutting handle of his six-shooter, but he did not lift the weapon out of the holster. He all at once doubted that he had the strength to hold the heavy gun level, to pull trigger.

Outside, the riders were already dismounting in a jumble of talk and strangely nervous laughter, and boots were tramping across hardpan earth towards the door. None of them, apparently, suspected that anyone was home; and from this, Emery suddenly derived his cue.

Leaving the bunk, he moved hurriedly across the room, found the curtain that chopped off one corner of the space for a closet. He slipped into this space, musty-smelling with the scent of sweat and wool, and he dropped the curtain to behind him. It was the narrowest of concealments. He put his shoulders to the rough board wall, and leaned there fighting the shakiness that was in him. After that the cabin door shoved open and men tramped into the room.

Steve Mallard's heavy tones were the first he heard. The Bar M boss sounded a little drunk, but probably just drunk enough to be dangerous. He said: "No rifles to bother us tonight, huh, Ross?"

There was a grunt of answer from Ross Boyden. A match was struck, its light gleaming faintly through the fabric of the cloth which shielded Emery. Mallard said: "Ain't there a lamp or nothing in this place?"

"Ain't nothing a white man would want," Boyden assured him, gruffly. A chair crashed as Mallard went blundering, looking for a light. For a moment he came very close to the curtain. Then Boyden called suddenly: "Here!" A lamp's chimney clinked, the light grew and steadied into a warm, golden glow. Steve Mallard grunted in satisfaction.

"Well, now we just set and wait." Accordingly, there was the scrape of chair legs being drawn back from the table. Someone righted the chair that had been knocked over. More feet were tramping up the front steps; the room was rapidly filling with men. "You left somebody outside to keep a look-out for that signal fire, Ross?" Mallard wanted to know.

The foreman said: "Sure."

"We lay here 'til it shows, then, and after that we ride. It ought to give Kingdom just about time to get his ranch cleared of men before we hit."

"He's in for a surprise, this night!"

A cork left a bottle-neck with a pop like a gun. Steve Mallard cried: "Now, go easy on that booze, damn it! You can get as drunk as you like after tonight's over, but I'm paying you to use your guns and by God I want to see you shootin' straight!"

There was silence for a moment following this outburst. Then Ross Boyden said, uneasily: "I still think we're doing this the dangerous way, Steve!"

"What other way was there—after that damned geologist's report busted any hope I had of getting water back on Bar M? I've bluffed this play through from the start, with a worthless hand. I've had old Kingdom on the hotseat thinking I meant to blow that slide, come hell or hot lead, when all the time I had no such intention because it wouldn't have done a bit of good.

"Tonight, the bluff pays off! A feint towards that slide, to draw Kingdom away from his ranch and into the hills—and then we ride in. And when someday that old range of mine beyond the Saddle dries up and blows away I won't give a damn—because I'll be sitting pretty on what used to be Crown!"

"It's all a matter of timing, I reckon. Hope nothing slips." Boyden still sounded dubious.

"Nothing will," answered Mallard, shortly. He added: "Give me a slug of that corn, Jay!" For a moment there was no talk, just the sound of men breathing and shifting, and beyond the open door the clink of a bronc's steel, and the murmur of a man's voice out there making an idle remark.

In his cubbyhole, Wade Emery had heard all this with a kind of numbness spreading through him. He knew, now, the pattern of tonight's treachery; he had a gun in his holster, and the author of that plan of destruction sat, unaware, not ten feet from where he crouched behind the shielding curtain. But when he reached across with right hand to pull the gun, the weapon seemed incredibly heavy. Sweat stood out upon his dark forehead, as he tried to find the strength to do what had to be done. But there was no strength, only a bullet-born weakness, and the yawning dark of waning consciousness.

"You're sure Rudebaugh will be taken care of?" Boyden asked.

"You worry too damn much!" his boss snorted. "I got Harris out of the way, didn't I, so as to be sure and not have a gun at my back? We haven't heard from Chuck Short, to make sure that Emery saddletramp is disposed of; but at least he's not here to bother us—"

At that moment, with final effort, Wade Emery got the gun out of its holster—and it slipped from numbed fingers, clattered to the floor. There was a startled cry, the sound of a chair tipping back as someone leaped up in that room yonder. But before any one of them could get to the cubbyhole, the hidden man toppled forward, loosely; the curtain tore away as his limp body struck it, and he went down in an unconscious sprawl full in view of the staring eyes of the Bar M riders.

CHAPTER XIV

Chuck Short had promised to send up a relief for the pair of Crown riders stationed at the slide, but now the second night was falling and no one came, and their supplies were growing short and so were their tempers. The silence of the peaks weighed oppressively. A cold star stood westward alone in the blue-black sky, and the creeping chill down from the higher snowfields bit through wool and set the body shivering.

Sid, to escape his companion's incessant complaining, had left the hollow in the rocks to take a look at things. "Don't be a damn fool!" Al called after him. "Bar M won't be monkeying around that slide after dark; and even if they did come, we'd hear them plain enough."

"I'm taking a look," repeated Sid, doggedly.

Balancing his rifle, he scrambled out of the hollow with its sheltered blaze and at once the wind hit him with chilling force. It rattled dry branches, and pushed against him as he moved forward. Then he was on hands and knees, clambering up over boulders and rock faces that still retained a little of the sun's warmth. Finally he poked rifle muzzle through a screen of brush and parted the branches, and looked out over a drop-off above the slide itself.

171

It was a black, ugly scar in the night, with the stars hanging close and glinting from snowfields and bare peaks. Sid settled down here, trying to forget the cold and his own empty belly, letting his glance work casually over that tumbled wreckage below him without any real thought of discovering anything. It must have been a half-hour later he suddenly pushed up to his elbows and crouched like that listening.

What had been a distant clink of metal on rock quickly grew to something more distinct—the unmistakable sounds of shod horses manoeuvring the tumbled slope somewhere beyond the slide. There were two, Sid thought. He studied the dark slope yonder until his eyes ached, trying to pick out some movement in that tumbled blackness.

He heard a scrambling behind him and Al Driscoe slid into position by his side. Al's voice was tense with excitement. "I heard something, Sid—"

"Yeah! You better get back there and get ready to torch that signal fire, Al. Looks like it's come!"

The other hesitated. "Maybe it's something else."

"Who else would be up here at a time like this? Maybe they know we're here, the way they're sneaking in!"

The sounds had ceased, and their own breathing and the breath of the night wind made the only noise now as, for tense moments, the pair searched out the far shadows beyond the slide. Sid's rifle scraped faintly on rock and wool as he slowly worked it around into position and laid the stock against his cheek.

Suddenly a match flared in a spot of yellow flame. Sid's rifle recoiled as his crooked finger took the trigger, and the lash of the weapon split the night's silence wide open, startlingly. The match dropped and guttered out. Next moment two guns answered from beyond the slide, the echoes of the shots rolling away across the dead stillness of the peaks.

Sid reached back, nudged Driscoe urgently with the edge of a palm. "Get going!" he whispered. "It's them all right. I'll try to keep them occupied—"

Al Driscoe went without another word. He slid down from the perch in the rocks, and when his boots hit level ground he began running, slipping and sliding in the loose rubble and the dark. Behind him the other Crown man's rifle was speaking again; and Al, with all the grumbling knocked out of him, put new speed into his running and soon was scrambling up to the wide, flat rock where the huge pile of brush for the bonfire had been laid.

He broke three matches in trembling fingers before one would light, and then he thrust it deep into the base of the pile. The brush had been soaked in kerosene, brought along for that purpose, and quickly it leaped into flame. Al Driscoe moved back from the sudden blistering heat of it. He watched the flames twisting and streaming sparks before the wash of the night wind. He thought: That ought to fetch them!

He could see, away below him, the lighted pattern of the town, and a few shining windows of scattered ranch houses. And, coming on the wind, the steady rattle of Sid's rifle.

One of those who had been waiting for the signal was Bart Yaeger. He was lounging under a cottonwood on one of the town's dark streets and, just about the moment he expected it, saw the bright dot of flame spring forth, high upon the side of the rimming hills.

At once, according to his cue, he shoved his humped shoulders away from the tree bole and hurried along the silent street to the house where Dick Rudebaugh lived alone. Lights showed in the windows, and the tiny yard was edged with bushes. Yaeger went to the front door, laid his fist against it; he was talking excitedly almost before the door swung open and Rudebaugh's great, shaggy head appeared limned in lamplight.

"Sheriff!" cried Bart. "You better come!" He turned, pointed to the spot of flame against the mountain wall. "That's Crown's signal that Bar M is trying to blow up the slide. It means a fight!"

Dick Rudebaugh came out onto the porch for

a squint at the signal fire. His scowl was fierce; his voice a deep bass rumble as he growled: "All right. I'll get my hat and coat!"

Yaeger was already starting away when the sheriff called him back. "Just a minute, Bart." Rudebaugh was studying him closely, with that uncomfortable blue glance that could read a man. He said, sharply: "Were you in on that thing this afternoon—moving Joel Harris to the jail against mine and the doc's orders?"

His tone was such that Yaeger swallowed nervously and was glad he could say honestly: "No, Sheriff. I never knew anything about that until it was over."

The lawman held him pinned with his eyes a moment longer; then he shrugged heavily and turned away again towards the door. Yaeger heard him muttering: "That's something I'll settle with Crown before I'm through!" He strode inside the little house and slammed the door.

At once Yaeger was out of the yard, and doubling over, he ran along behind the bushes towards the back. The sheriff had a small barn and corral here, where he kept his saddle-horse, and it was this way he would be coming when he left the house. Yaeger was hardly in position, six-gun ready, when Dick Rudebaugh came tramping outside in such a hurry that he left the lamp burning in the house behind him.

Yaeger fired one shot. It was a good one, and

it took the sheriff's thick body with a force that stopped Dick Rudebaugh in mid-stride. He reached one hand around towards his back, and then with a groan broke and went down in a solid sprawl. His hat slewed off. He hit the path and lay there twisting a little, and Yaeger could vaguely see the face turned towards him.

Somewhere, on the echo of the shot, a voice yelled. Bart Yaeger was already up, with six-gun back in holster, and he was moving away from there through darkness and brush. He had left the scene well behind him before the first man came running into the yard to stumble across the body of the dying sheriff.

Terry Franz was giving Chris and Jim their supper when the summons came. Face gone white, she stammered some answer to the man who brought the news and then she hurried out back, where her father was sitting on the steps with his hat off and his shoulders slumped limply against the wall, eyes closed, letting the night breeze ruffle his thinning hair. "Pop!" she cried. She went down on her knees beside him, took the wasted shoulders in her hands. "It's Dick Rudebaugh. He's been shot—he may be dying. Hurry!"

The doctor turned slowly and stared at her as though not understanding; but then the import of her words struck home and at once he was floundering to his feet. "My God!" he cried, over and over. "Not old Dick—it can't be!"

"I'll get your hat, Pop. And your bag."

Always, after one of his drinking bouts, William Franz was left a trembling and nearly helpless wreck of a man. Terry knew him well in this condition. She put his hat on for him, but the hand he reached for the bag was shaking so she doubted he could even carry it.

"Wait a minute, Pop," she said, suddenly. "I'm going along."

Chris and Jim could look out for themselves for a while. Terry took her father's arm and with the bag of instruments in her own hand went beside his shambling, shrunken frame through the dark streets.

Once, Doctor Franz said: "Terry, what star is that?"

She looked, and frowned. "I don't think it's a star, Pop! It—it looks like a fire, a whale of a big fire, up on the mountainside." She continued to stare at it after that, not understanding, and wondering what it could mean.

They found the sheriff's house with all its doors thrown open, and lights in the kitchen and the front room. Somebody had carried Dick Rudebaugh inside and laid him out on the old sofa, that was hump-backed and shapeless with loosened springs. But the dying man was all alone when Terry and her father entered, and he lay and groaned with his sharp blue eyes turned up until all they could see of them was the milky whites.

One look, and Doctor Franz shook his head. "No use—it's no use, Terry! He's done for!" The doctor bit a trembling lip, and suddenly his weak eyes filled with moisture that he did not try to hide. Dick Rudebaugh had been his friend, one of the few who accepted William Franz as an equal and liked him for what he was—or in spite of what he was. Grief-stricken, the doctor could only drag a chair beside the couch now and sit down beside the sheriff, whose breathing was a harsh and rasping sound in the room. The mouth worked on mumbled, unheard words; the lips were dry, and William Franz said to his daughter: "Quick, girl! Get him something to drink—"

She hurried into the kitchen, returned with a dipper of water. The sheriff had his eyes open now and Franz was saying, quickly: "Who did it? Do you know who shot you, Dick?"

Rudebaugh was trying to answer. Terry stepped in and lifted his great, shaggy head and put the dipper to his lips; he got down a couple of swallows and when she let him back he gasped: "Yaeger! I—saw him as he ran—"

"Bart Yaeger!" exclaimed the doctor. And to Terry: "Remember that, girl!"

Sweat stood on the face of the dying man, and his face told of his suffering. The doctor said:

"Give me a hand to turn him a little, Terry." They dragged a groan from the sheriff doing it, and revealed the ugly mess the bullet had made. "It smashed a rib," said William Franz, "and followed around to lodge against the spine. That's what's torturing him! But if I could cut that slug out, take away the pressure of it—" He snapped bony fingers. "Quick! My scalpel, from the bag!"

"Yes, Pop!"

He took the knife from her, turned again to the couch. But then, as he bent over the body of his friend, she saw him hesitate and straighten slowly. He was looking at his hands, at the tremble whisky had put into them. She could tell from the tightness of his features that her father was battling with himself, fighting to force strength and sturdiness into those ruined tools. Suddenly then he flung the blade from him clear across the room, and he dropped into the chair behind him and buried his face against his useless, shaking fingers. The dying man's breathing was coming harder and sharper now, each breath a groan.

"I could have helped him!" sobbed the doctor, in a frenzy. "I could have eased his last minutes. But now he's got to die in torment, because—"

"Don't, Pop!" exclaimed Terry, putting an arm consolingly across his thin shoulders. But it was slim comfort and she left him and went slowly across the room, picked up the knife he had flung away. As she came up with it in her hand she saw

179

the yellow envelope on a table against the wall, and beside it a telegram. A name caught her eye and she read the brief message twice before quite comprehending what it meant. When she did, she took the telegram, on sudden impulse, and thrust it into a pocket of her dress.

. . . And finally—an eternity later, perhaps—it was all over; and still William Franz sat motionless beside the body of the man who had been his friend. Sight of her father's grief and self-loathing touched Terry Franz, and it hurt. She went into the kitchen. There on a shelf she found a half-empty bottle of bourbon, and she poured some of this into a tumbler and went with it into the other room. "Here, Pop," she said gently. "Maybe this will help a little."

He sat up slowly, looked at her and at the liquor, a dullness in his weak blue eyes. Suddenly he slapped the glass from her fingers with the edge of a palm, knocked it crashing to the floor. The liquor made a wet smear on the worn carpet. William Franz stood up then, and walked to the open door; he put a hand on her shoulder, in passing, and gave it a gentle squeeze, and she understood his apology for that sharp action and accepted it.

Looking out at the night, William Franz repeated suddenly: "Bart Yaeger! We've got to find Lee Ball, and tell him."

"We will, Pop," said Terry.

• • •

At that moment Lee Ball was in the Clover Leaf with an elbow on the bar and a spur cocked over the footrail. He had had a few drinks, and was having one more. That was to wash out some of the bad taste left by Dick Rudebaugh's tongue lashing, that took place when the sheriff came back to the office that afternoon and learned about his deputy's opening the jail on Chuck Short's orders, and locking Joel Harris inside.

Crown, Dick had shouted in that thunderous voice of his, did not run the sheriff's office whatever Thad Kingdom and his bully-boss might think to the contrary. If Harris died from his maltreatment at the hands of Chuck Short's men, he would damn well hale the whole Crown outfit into court for manslaughter—and Lee himself had better look out for his job! There had been plenty more of the same; but it played out finally after the sheriff had a look at his prisoner and found Harris was not in much worse shape for his manhandling. In fact, the man's battered knee had done so well under the doctor's care that Rudebaugh said he would leave Harris in his cell now that he was there. The prisoner would be well enough for trial in a few days more.

So it blew over, after all, but as soon as Rudebaugh was through with him Lee had headed for the Clover Leaf. He was there now, and a little unsteady, when Bart Yaeger swaggered in.

Yaeger had been looking for Lee Ball, and he came over and hooked an elbow on the mahogany. They were pretty much alone. No one else caught Yaeger's words as he murmured: "Heard about your boss?"

"No," grunted Lee, thickly. "What about him?"

"Dead!"

The deputy reeled a little, against the hand he put out to clasp the edge of the bar as he blinked under the impact of this. He repeated the word, foolishly.

"A six-gun bullet out of the dark," went on Yaeger, finding wolfish pleasure in the effect of this news. "Somebody that didn't like sheriffs. Somebody that didn't like lawmen," he added, meaningly.

Lee Ball looked at his whisky glass. He picked it up, set it down again, spilling a little. His face had gone ashen and there was a faint film of sweat across his cheeks.

"Another thing you probably don't know," went on Yaeger. "Tonight's showdown. Bar M is moving in—and Crown is out! Things are apt to be kind of mixed up around these parts, the next few hours. Sort of a bad time for lawmen. You know what I mean?"

The deputy flicked out a narrow tongue and moistened his lips with it. He said, in a sort of croak: "Yeah, I—guess I know." He pushed away from the bar suddenly. "Thanks, Bart. Thanks for the tip!"

"S'all right, you're welcome," grunted Yaeger. As the other moved away Yaeger turned to the bar and caught the tender's eye, held up his finger for a drink. He knew where Lee Ball was heading—to find a horse, and ride. Everything was set. Yaeger's part of the big job was finished.

The law had been disposed of; now the plum was ripe, and waiting to drop straight into Steve Mallard's ready hands.

CHAPTER XV

Bar M rode in easily and without great haste, a dozen shadowy riders strung out along the trail that dipped down the western flank of the Saddle. There was no one to oppose them, no sound except that of their own horses, and an occasional comment that went back and forth along the line. When they came to sight of Crown headquarters, they found the buildings aglow with lamplight but there was no movement. Steve Mallard reined in a minute, his men grouped behind him, to study the scene and make sure.

Mallard was feeling more confident all the time. Once he had been certain of everything except Wade Emery; now on that score too his mind was at rest. All his plans in fact had worked so smoothly to this point that it seemed a good, sure token of success. He only smiled when Ross Boyden said: "Looks quiet enough down there. But it could be a trap—"

"It's no trap. Old Kingdom and all his crew are into the hills by now. Maybe the cook's left, but you can bet that's about all."

"What about the girl?"

Steve Mallard considered. "Yes, keep your eye out for her. Don't hurt her—I aim to talk business with her before this thing is over." He added: "Let's go!"

They found no resistance at all. The cook was there, and in the bunkhouse a puncher who had hurt his leg in a spill and couldn't ride. When this pair looked into the blunt ends of Bar M six-shooters, even their curses fell to silence. At Steve Mallard's orders the old cook set to work at once hitching a team to buckboard, and he piled blankets in back to ease the jolt for his hurt friend. "Take the quickest trail out of this range," said the Bar M boss, "and don't look back. Crown is through; and nothing that was ever Crown will stay here after tonight."

Lynne Kingdom, he learned, had ridden away sometime before supper. This was just as well, for he was left now with a free hand to work his will. He looked around him, at the big barn and the corrals and the tall white house. He said: "Burn it!"

The foreman stared. "Everything, Steve?" He too glanced at the big house. "That's a nice layout. You could use it later."

"Burn it!" repeated the Bar M boss, flatly. "We'll build new. I want no part of Crown left standing." And as Boyden shrugged thick shoulders and turned away to give the necessary orders, he called after him: "If there's any stock in the barn, run 'em out before you put the torch to it. I'm not warring against calves and horses!"

"Right, Steve."

. . . The seasoned timbers of these wooden

buildings made excellent kindling. Steve Mallard stood apart and watched the flames grow, bright tongues that licked and devoured. An exultation filled him as the sparks streamed skyward, marking the passage of an old order and the induction of a new. The growing, dancing light showed his black-browed face, and the full mouth was smiling now, no longer sullen.

Their work done finally, and driven away by the heat, the Bar M crew gathered around their boss and watched the burning silently, with that awe fire always instills in men. Every building had taken the torch, in its own separate bier of streaming sparks. Satisfied at last that the fires were beyond quenching, Mallard turned to the horse cavvy and waited in saddle for his men to mount while he studied the blazing outline of the big house and heard the crackling of the flames. The roof of the cookshack crashed inward.

"Leave a man," Mallard told Boyden suddenly, as the latter reined over to his side. "I gave Chuck Short the job of disposing of old Kingdom during the confusion up yonder in the hills. Just in case he misses, it would be a good idea to have someone spotted here. Then, if Kingdom gets this far, we'll know he won't get any farther." He added: "That dark slope yonder would make a good place to watch for him, and it will be an easy rifle shot, against the fire."

Boyden nodded and spurred away to set his

ambush. The man told off fell out of line and headed for the dark, brushy slope facing the house; and Ross Boyden put his bronc into a gallop and brought it even with Mallard's again. "What now, boss?" he asked. "Where from here?"

"To town," the Bar M owner answered, and his voice sounded smug and pleased. "To town, and sit and wait for the payoff!"

Jessie Ferguson's father was by nature a silent man, and the presence of Lynne Kingdom at his table served to still his tongue even more than normally. It was awe of her name and family position that did this. The Scotsman spoke seldom during the meal, addressed her as "Miss Kingdom" whenever he did, and his manner was stilted and touched with not a little hostility. Crown was respected by its lesser neighbours, but it could not be said that they felt any affection for it.

Lynne sensed this reticence in her host, she knew it well from past experience, and it did little to help her mood this evening, or to ease the smouldering feeling of resentment against her father. She wished now she had not come here. Hampered by her own troubles, she found it doubly hard to beat against the reserve she felt in the people about her; and only the daughter of the family seemed really at her ease and happy her friend had dropped in for the evening.

Jessie's bright chatter ran aimlessly across the strained silence of the meal, and brought no echo of response.

The stolid country meal of boiled beef, potatoes and coffee was nearly finished before John Ferguson made one of his few independent observations of the evening. "Funny thing," he remarked, as he stirred his cup, "about that fire up on the hill—"

The clatter of Lynne's fork chiming against her plate as she dropped it brought all their eyes on her. She echoed: "A fire?"

"Why, yes, Miss Kingdom. I saw it just before I came in to supper. I don't reckon it'll spread, though, because there ain't much growth that far up over timberline. It was pretty close to the slide, I figure."

Already Lynne's chair was scraping as she came hastily to her feet. She hardly heard Mrs. Ferguson's startled question. She got the door open, hurried out to the shallow porch. The signal fire must have burnt itself out, because there was no break in the darkness of the hill rim. But some nameless prompting drew her to the railing, and at what she saw leaning from this new position, a gasp broke from her and Lynne's hands tightened on the rail.

Crown was burning! From the spread of the flames, every building at the home ranch must have gone under the torch. Lynne could only stare, unbelieving, for long thundering seconds. And then, quickly, she was down the steps and running towards the corral even as the Fergusons came hurrying out of the house calling to her.

She heard their startled exclamations as they too saw the fire. By that time Lynne had the corral gate open and Prince came trotting to his name. He still wore the light saddle, and the carbine was in the boot, and quickly Lynne found the stirrup and stepped up, hands trembling as she took the reins.

Up on the steps of the house, Jessie Ferguson was calling anxiously to her friend, but Lynne did not even answer. The little pinto straightened out into a gallop and quickly the Ferguson place was left behind, and there was the wind against her face as she drove straight across the flats towards her burning home.

The white house blazing upon its hill made a beacon that she knew must be seen all down the sloping length of this mountain valley. Men would be staring in awe, watching the sparks streaming upward; and yet she had a sudden, sickening realization that they would do no more than watch. Lynne had long realized that her father was not liked, that Crown itself inspired only fear and jealousy among its neighbours. Even the Fergusons, in spite of the friendship between herself and Jessie, could not be counted on for any help now that disaster had struck the Kingdom ranch.

As she came in towards the burning buildings and saw how deserted they were, the truth struck home with a numbing force and left her filled with a greater loneliness than she had ever known. She felt crushingly her own impotence, as well. She dragged her pinto to a halt atop a knoll behind the house and slipped down from saddle, having a need for firm ground beneath her trembling legs.

Here, the dance of the flames made a faint warmth upon her flushed, wind-numbed cheeks. The roof of the barn went with a crash and a smother of fire and swirling sparks. She could see there was not a soul about the place, and guessed her father and his riders had been tolled up into the hills, to the dreaded summons of the signal.

Lynne knew small hope of saving anything, but nevertheless she dropped reins here and went forward, blindly, down the slope where wind rushing in towards the fire bowed the grasses and whispered in brush. Without knowing quite why, she slipped the carbine from her saddle boot and took that with her. Then, almost at the foot of the slope, she saw that which made her thankful she had obeyed the half-felt impulse.

He was a vague, black shape against the fire— just the outline of his tall Stetson and the jut of a rifle barrel canted at the stars. The wind had covered her approach and the man did not hear her coming until that same instant, when she was almost upon him, and then he was whirling with a grunt of surprise and the rifle in his hands snapped into position.

There was no time to think. She had her own carbine and she caught her footing and stepped back, starlight streaking on metal as she swung the weapon by the barrel. She felt the jar of it when the wooden stock connected at the end of its flat, wild arc, heard the smash as the wood splintered. Then with a groan the man was toppling and Lynne dropped her ruined rifle, both hands pressed in horror against her face.

He lay silently at her feet, and somewhere along the slope a horse stamped. Terror gripped her tensed body until she decided that the horse must belong to the man she had dropped. Nerving herself then, she moved forward and went to a knee in the dew-damp grass. Searching fingers found the rough wool of a shirt; there was a sack of tobacco in the pocket, and that meant the man must have matches on him. She located these in the unbuttoned vest, and struck one alight with shaking fingers.

It was a Bar M rider. He lay on his back, mouth drooped slackly, blood on his head where Lynne's frantic blow had struck. But he was not dead.

Horror gave way to relief that she had not killed a man, and then all this was swept away by quick fury. Steve Mallard had burned her father's ranch! She had known this, really, all along, but here was the proof. Mallard had struck here and at the slide, simultaneously.

Suddenly she came to her feet, knowing what there was to do. No hope of saving anything of the burning ranch—the big white house was a gutted skeleton now, its bones showing against the fury of the flames within. But she had a prisoner, and a prisoner could be made to talk. She would take him to town, to Dick Rudebaugh. The sheriff would know what to do with such evidence.

Getting the weight of the unconscious man across his saddle was a job that proved almost too much for her. Yet she accomplished it, and trembling with exhaustion led his horse with its still burden up the slope to where Prince was waiting. As she came into saddle she heard a crash from below which she knew must be the caving of the walls of her fire-gutted home.

Resolutely, she would not look back. It was better to be riding, to have some purpose and something certain to accomplish. Find Dick Rudebaugh! What came afterwards, she did not know nor did she think beyond it. She fastened upon this single idea that had grown to an obsession and the one stabilizing source of strength in a black night of horror and uncertainty.

So strong was this emotion that it stunned her

to any other thoughts, and she rode in a numb suspension of rationality until she looked about with a shock to find the lights of town showing around her. Where would she be most apt to find Dick Rudebaugh? At his home, likely. But no, there were lights in his office at the courthouse, and with her heart singing its relief she headed there directly and swung down, tying both horses to the scarred railing of the veranda. The man across the saddle was still unconscious. She left him there as she hurried up the steps.

The veranda was empty. Lynne crossed it with quick stride, stepped into the dark hallway. Lamplight spilled on the wall facing the opened door of the sheriff's office; Rudebaugh's name was already forming on her lips as she turned in there, but the word died unspoken. She halted on the threshold, staring, as the man in the sheriff's chair wheeled quickly to face her. It was Steve Mallard.

She could not speak. Surprise in the man's face quickly died and gave way to pleasure that twisted the full lips into a smirk. Mallard's stocky frame came up out of the chair then and he said: "Looking for someone? Rudebaugh, maybe? You won't find him, Miss Kingdom. He's dead. Murdered!"

The terrible word struck through to her, and she repeated it soundlessly.

Expression unchanged, Mallard said: "You're

shocked at that? You must be—you're very pale. Let me get a chair for you."

He stepped quickly and brought one from a corner, placing it near the desk. She shook her head, tried for words that would not come.

"You had better have a seat, Miss Kingdom." And now Mallard's tone had altered subtly, hardened. "There's worse news!"

She knew suddenly what he meant. Her eyes on him, she stumbled forward as though groping her way, and gripped the back of the chair he had set for her until the knuckles of the brown hands were white. "My father?"

Mallard shrugged, and a hint of irritation was in his frown. "So you can take it standing! All right," and with a quick move he slammed the door and then went back to his swivel chair, dropped into it and tilted back to look squarely at the girl. "Miss Kingdom," he said bluntly, "I'm not a man to go down without fighting. And it turns a man sick inside to see the range he's fought for drying out before his eyes, and the cattle that represent every cent he owns facing the surest kind of starvation. I'd been less than a man if I hadn't fought back! You can't blame me entirely."

Fire flashed behind her brown eyes; already anger was working through the numbness of shock. "So you fight back by striking down your neighbours. Just because my father didn't want you tampering with that slide—as though it were his fault, to begin with!"

"Call it an act of God," grunted Mallard, heavily. He went on: "I despised Thad Kingdom! It's a cruel thing to say to you, but I'm trying to explain. Your father was an unscrupulous, selfish, and hateful man—and I have no compunction at all about killing him, or taking away from him what he stole, himself, from other and better men. I do regret, though, having to hurt you at the same time."

Her eyes flashed scornfully. Mallard, reaching into an inner pocket of his coat, drew out two pieces of paper. One, she saw, was a bill of sale; the other a cheque. He laid them both upon the desk, within her reach. He said coldly: "I could have Crown for the taking, and I think you know it. Instead, I'm offering to buy you out at a fair and reasonable price. All you need to do is sign this bill of sale."

"I'll go to the law!"

He shook his head. "I don't think so. There is no law in this west slope country now, and if you brought it in from outside you'd never prove a case against me—not over things that happened in confusion and the dark. You know that!"

Lynne was thinking of her prisoner; there was evidence—Then, the full truth of what Mallard said struck her. Because she was Crown, she had no friends. And without friends or help she was powerless. Suddenly she knew that Steve Mallard had this whole thing figured correctly.

Moving woodenly, she came around the chair towards the desk. The figures written on the cheque in Mallard's bold scrawl met her eye. It was, as he said, a very decent offer. Very fair indeed, for a ranch that had been humbled as Crown had been tonight—its owner killed, its riders scattered, its buildings put under the torch. Unscrupulous as Mallard was, he yet was being generous in his triumph; and it was more, she had to admit, than could ever have been said of her father in the years when he was building Crown upon the ruins of other, smaller ranchers.

She lowered herself into the chair, took the pen Mallard had placed for her beside the bill of sale. She had made the first stroke upon the paper when Ross Boyden came bursting into the room with excited glance searching out his chief. "It's Crown!" he exclaimed. "They've just ridden in. Thad Kingdom's heading them!"

Unbelieving joy that swept through Lynne Kingdom died under the ferocity of Mallard's look. "So Short crossed up!" he growled. "Well, this makes no difference!" The swivel chair creaked as he came out of it, turning to his fore-man. "Take this girl and put her some place where she'll be safe. With her for a talking point, I'll deal with old Kingdom directly. And I think it will be a pleasure!"

CHAPTER XVI

It had not proved as simple as Chuck Short expected, putting a bullet into Thad Kingdom. There'd been no chance, up under the slide, with the Crown men bunched together around their chief waiting for the attack that failed to come. Then, after someone spotted Crown burning down below and they started the slow and painful haul down from timberline, the opportunity never seemed just right. Once or twice, riding behind his boss, Short had had his six-gun in his hand and levelled at the narrow shoulders of the tall shape in front of him. But it was not the time, for the other Crown riders were strung out behind him and they would know. And suppose he missed?

After that they hit the level lands and the chance was gone.

They delayed only a few moments at Crown, while Thad Kingdom let the sight of his burned and lost home engrave itself in his eyes in letters of hatred, and bring a torrent of profanity and foul language pouring from the old man's tight, bloodless lips. Now they were flagging into town, grimly silent as they swung down before the Blue Chip and snubbed reins to the toothmarked tie-poles. They were like that when Steve Mallard himself came striding out to the veranda of the courthouse across the street, his short and compact body silhouetted against the light in the window of the sheriff's office. His voice called across the dust: "Kingdom!"

The men from Crown turned sharply, and Mallard stood alone on the courthouse steps facing them. Old Thad Kingdom, head and shoulders towering gauntly above his men, cried: "You! I'll shoot you like a mad dog!"

"No you won't!" answered Steve Mallard, quietly. His gun was in its holster, and it stayed there. "You won't, because your daughter's safety means more than that to you."

Old Kingdom echoed: "My daughter?"

Mallard jerked his head. "Come over," he invited, shortly, "and we'll talk about it. But come alone!"

Boot leather squealed as he turned abruptly and, before Kingdom could choke out another word, strode heavily back through the dark door. The old man stood as though thunderstruck, faded eyes blazing. Someone muttered: "It's a trick!"

"Sure," said another. "Don't let him bluff you, Thad!"

It was as though old Kingdom did not hear them. Under his breath he said: "I've got to know!" He seemed to think this over, and then he nodded and said it again in the same dead voice: "I've got to know!"

When they started to follow he waved them back, and then in an uncertain group the Crown riders stood near their horses and watched his lath-lean shape move across the dust and, mechanically, up the three steps to the courthouse. Short, watching with the others, knew a sudden easing of anxiety. Steve Mallard had sounded very confident. Maybe he had an ace up his sleeve. Maybe it was going to be all right after all, despite Short's failure to follow orders.

There were two others in the sheriff's office with Mallard. Ross Boyden and Bart Yaeger. Old Kingdom passed over the latter almost as though not recognizing his traitorous hand. Thad's look went instead to Mallard, who was tilted back in the sheriff's chair, his fingers idly twirling a small, broad-brimmed riding hat. "You recognize this, I suppose," said Mallard. "There are initials inside—"

"Don't bother!" old Kingdom grunted. "Just tell me what you've done with her."

The Bar M boss shook his head. "I haven't hurt her, and I don't intend to—if you'll be sensible." He tossed the hat to the desk, and picked up the bill of sale that already bore the first few strokes of Lynne Kingdom's signature. "Just sign this. In return I'll give you back your girl, and I'll let you have twelve hours to be away from this range for good. Moreover—yes!" He brought

201

out the cheque book he had offered Lynne. "I'll throw this in, as well, though I don't know why I should when I know damn well you stole Crown in the first place!"

Thad Kingdom's face was a mask. He came stiffly to the chair by the desk, folded his lean strength upon it and took the bill of sale and the cheque. His glance flickered briefly as he saw the sizeable amount of the latter. Then he put it aside and read the bill of sale through, carefully.

"You'll find no loopholes," Mallard told him, drily. "Once you sign, Crown is really gone! And you'll never steal it back, either."

Kingdom's eyes came up quickly, burned levelly across at his enemy. "All right!" he gritted. "You got me over a barrel. There's only one way you could make me lie down and take this—and you've found that way! Bring my daughter here, and I'll sign. But not before!"

Their glances locked and held for a long moment, the triumph in Steve Mallard's tempered by a caution of this beaten enemy. Then, briefly, he turned to Bart Yaeger, whose hump-shouldered frame leaned against the edge of the office door. "Go get her, Bart."

"Okay, Steve!"

Bart swung along the dark hall, to the jingle of keys on the ring in his bony hand. He climbed the narrow stairs, shoved a key into the lock of the iron-bound door opening off the first landing.

As he swung that door open, stale, trapped heat breathed at him from the block of cells.

A single lamp suspended from the ceiling gave dim, shadowed light. Yaeger saw the white face of Joel Harris in his cell near the door, and went quickly past down the centre corridor to its farthest end, near the windows where the heat was not so stifling, and here he fitted a key and swung a barred door wide. "Come on out," he ordered.

Lynne Kingdom moved into the light, her dark hair dishevelled, stubborn jaw set firmly. Yaeger could not quite meet the scorn in her eyes. He hunched his shoulders, motioned toward the big door up front. "Your dad's ready to sign," he muttered. "Come on."

When he moved to put a hand on her arm she shook him off and went stiffly along the corridor, with a quick tapping of boot-heels. But just short of the iron-bound door she halted, suddenly, turning to face him as he came up with her. In the poor light he detected nothing in her eyes, in the tense set of her body. "Have they hurt my father?" she demanded, facing him. "Have they, Bart?"

"Naw!" He said it impatiently, and moved to urge her on outside the cell room. He was like that, close to her, when she suddenly threw her weight against him and shoved. Going backwards he struck iron bars, fighting for balance; then an

203

arm shot out from behind him to crook about his neck, jerk his head back hard. At the same moment the gun slipped from Yaeger's holster. He felt it go. He let out one choked bellow, a startled cry for help, before his own gun-barrel came against his skull solidly and he went limp against the bars.

Joel Harris cried: "Get his keys, Lynne!"

Quickly she plucked them from the floor where they had fallen and with shaking fingers tried them, one by one, until she found the right key for Joel's cell. Bart Yaeger's body slid loosely down as Joel let go his hold through the bars. When the door swung wide Joel stepped out quickly with Yaeger's gun in his hand, and Lynne went into his arms weeping from nervous exhaustion.

"Good girl!" he grunted. "You got him neatly!" But next moment he had to put her away from him because boots were pounding on the narrow stairs. Joel snatched the key ring, limped to the big door and clanged it shut, turned the lock just as those outside hit the landing. He pulled the girl to one side, away from the narrow window in the door, shoved her against the wall beside it.

Someone on the landing hit the door, and there was a grunt of alarm when it failed to open. A voice cried: "Bart! What's wrong in there?"

Eyes haggard, hair plastered over sweaty forehead, Joel shouted back: "This is Harris speaking! I've got Yaeger's keys, and his gun.

Get back or I'll put a bullet through the window!"

A scramble away from the door was followed by a moment's tense silence. Then more feet sounded on the stairs and Steve Mallard's voice came, harsh and a little breathless. "What the hell are you trying to do? Hold me up?"

"What I said goes for you!" Joel retorted. "You had Yaeger try to frame me, I figure. That gives me a score to settle!"

It was a long second before Mallard's voice came again. "Don't be a fool!" he said then. "Open that door and you can walk out of here a free man, and no one will be hurt. It's my promise on that!"

"You'd better take it, Joel!" There was a dull edge to Lynne's whisper. "You can't buck them all—just one gun against them! And I think he can at least be trusted to keep his word."

Joel shook his head. "I know what I'm doing. He can't make us come out—and as long as we stay here we can keep Mallard from getting what he wants. A stalemate is better than defeat!"

"But it's not your fight, Joel! If he has Crown, he'll be satisfied. I know that! Don't—don't risk everything, just for the sake of the Kingdoms. We aren't worth it!"

"I know what I'm doing!" he repeated. And lifting his voice he called to Steve Mallard: "Go to hell, Mallard! See if you can make your deal with Thad, without giving up your hostage. Because you can't make one with me!"

Through the silence, he could imagine the baffled fury written on Steve Mallard's heavy, sullen face.

Trailing his chief down the narrow stairs, Ross Boyden had an idea. "This building ought to burn easy. What do you say, Steve?"

"Fool!" growled Mallard. "I don't fight women—and the girl is not to be hurt. If it was just Harris, I wouldn't give a damn; he could stay in there and rot. And Bart Yaeger, too. It was his stupidity got us into this mess!"

When he strode into the sheriff's office again, he found that Thad Kingdom had left. Mallard was not surprised. Old Thad would know Mallard was stopped, for the time being, because of the determination of that fool in the cellblock. Until Mallard could produce his daughter, Kingdom would not sign. That was the long and short of it.

"Well, what are we going to do?" demanded Boyden, not at all liking the turn things were taking.

"Do?" Mallard dropped into the chair by the desk. "Exactly nothing!

"There's no food or water up there, and you can imagine how hot that second floor must get in the middle of the day. Even a mean old devil like Kingdom can't see his own kid go through too much of that. It's my guess he'll break first. And when he breaks, he'll sign—and that will end it!"

Ross Boyden scowled at the floor. "I damn well hope it's soon!" he muttered.

Thad Kingdom walked across the dust to his saloon, and at the door he turned sharply and looked at the hitchrack a second time. It was empty! The fact had registered only slowly through the tumult in the old man's brain, and he could not quite grasp it. Nor could he understand the silence of the bar-room behind the swinging doors.

He shoved them wide, went through. Buck was at his place behind the mahogany, and this side of it Chuck Short lounged with his whang-braided hat shoved back from thinning hair, boot cocked over the brass rail and a half-filled glass in his fingers. There was no one else. Old Thad's jaw thrust suspiciously, the turkey jowls standing out red and raw as he surveyed the empty room. "Where the hell is my crew?" he thundered.

Chuck Short straightened slowly, a smile touching his hard mouth. "Looks like they're gone, Thad!"

Old Kingdom looked at his foreman, not understanding. Short spotted a bar bottle and took it in one big hand, snagged two glasses with the other. He jerked his head towards a table at the rear of the room. "Come and sit a minute and I'll tell you all about it, Thad. You look like you could use a drink."

He went straight back there. Kingdom hesitated, scowling, and then he followed stiffly and kicking a chair out of the way leaned across the table at Short, who had already slouched into a chair. "What are you drivelling about?" he demanded, fiercely. "Where are my riders?"

"Set down!" barked Chuck Short. No one had ever spoken this way to old Thad before, and automatically he obeyed; but his face was thunderous under the white, flat-topped hat. Calmly Short poured whisky into a glass, shoved it across the table, and filled his own again. He had waited for this moment, and he was stretching it out.

He picked up his glass, set it down. Kingdom's remained where it was, untouched. Looking at his boss, levelly, Chuck Short gave it to him then: "You're through, Thad! Your crew's pulled out on you, to a man. You haven't a friend in the world—not a soul that likes you well enough to lift a hand to save your ranch, or your dirty, selfish hide." He shook his head, slowly, and smiled. "While you had power you ran things and to hell with anyone else. Now you're absolutely, teetotally alone!"

Fury blazed in the old man's eyes, made his lips tremble. "My crew rode out—and you didn't stop them?"

"Stop them?" Short laughed harshly, lifted his drink and tossed it off. He shook his head above the empty glass. "Hell, Thad, I told them to go!

One or two almost wanted to stick, but I talked 'em out of it. I made 'em see it was safer."

Kingdom's face was colourless. "You dirty—traitorous—"

The other only grinned. "I've taken enough off the Kingdoms. You can go to hell! I thought once I was sweet on that girl of yours, but she can go to hell, too—and roast up in that oven of a cellblock as long as you figure on letting her. I got a better deal with Steve Mallard; now, there's a gent a man enjoys working for!"

He stood up, casually. "Well—" His heavy-lidded gaze flickered towards the shot glass standing full at Kingdom's fingers. "Enjoy your drink!"

He turned and rang his spurs towards the swinging doors. He was half way there when the roar of the gun boomed out in the empty room. It jerked him up, amazement and pain tightening his face. He tried to get around; made a move toward his holstered gun but only touched the handle. Then the floppy hat dropped from his head and Chuck Short went down on top of it, dead before he hit.

Thad Kingdom slid the smoking gun back into holster without looking at it, his fierce brown eyes peering through drift of powdersmoke at the blood fouling the back of Short's coat. Then his eyes sought Buck's behind the mahogany. The bartender's eyes glittered wide with horror, but there was no change in old Kingdom's hatchet face. "Drag the skunk outside!" he ordered. "Throw him in the gutter!"

"Okay, Thad!" Quickly, Buck moved to obey. Thad Kingdom lifted the glass of whisky, then, and took it at a single swallow. The hand, he noticed with contempt, trembled a little. He filled the glass again, and spilled a part of the liquor on the green baize top.

Buck, returning with his grisly job completed, looked at Thad drinking like that after calmly shooting a man in the back. Revulsion shook him. And a strangely incongruous thought crossed the barkeeper's mind: Why—he's sitting at Doc Franz's old table!

CHAPTER XVII

The sun came up into a sky untouched by clouds, and at noon it stood interminably at the high zenith of the heavens, its blaze making a dazzle of the river's face, a smear of the red roof of the bandstand in the park beside it, a shimmer from the dust of the streets. No wind stirred the dust, or moved in the drooping tree heads. At Crown, the ashes of what had been a once-proud ranch scarred the earth blackly. The gleaming flanks of old Baldy reared glistening above the lower hills.

Toward the end of that breathless day, a slight hint of breeze moved in across the sloping miles from the Saddle's high bank, but it died again as the sun dipped toward the western rim. But then, at least, the direct blast of heat was lifted from the land and evening shadows began creeping out upon the valley floor. Sunset colours faded to smoke, and the stars burned higher in their spangled mesh across the deepening sky. The first day of Steve Mallard's rule was over.

Doctor William Franz sat quite alone in the kitchen of his house, a meal half eaten before him, the window at his elbow opened wide upon the sultry heat. The two youngest children were in bed, and Terry had disappeared somewhere; he knew some of the torment that was in her mind, and did not hold her to account for her comings and goings. The doctor himself was deep in black musings—so engrossed that a silent step beyond the outer door, the careful opening of the screen, were slow to register.

When he did turn sharply, his visitor was already inside the room with shoulders leaned tiredly against the door casing, and one hand cautiously near the forward-jutting butt of his holstered six-gun. The doctor came slowly to his feet. His first thought was that this stranger would be one of Mallard's gunfighters, sent here for some reason to dispose of him; no man knew, in the grim uncertainty of the new order of things here, exactly how he stood with the new masters of Kingdom's shattered range.

But this one before him did not have the look of the Bar M gunmen, or the triumphant swagger with which they walked the streets of the fear-ridden town. He looked tired, and haggard, and his clothes were foul with grime and the caking of dried blood. His voice when he spoke was unsteady, but with grim determination behind it. "You're Doctor Franz?"

The other nodded, waiting.

"I want to see the man you've got here. And quick!"

This told Doctor Franz it was one of Mallard's men after all, for it was a Bar M gunman he was tending in that front bedroom, now—one who had been brought in last night, unconscious, with his head a bloody mess. An ear had been practically torn off, and there were stitches to take and maybe a fractured skull. According to confused reports, the man had been found that way, draped across the back of his own saddlehorse. Someone had given him a terrific clout with a club or rifle stock, from which he had not yet regained consciousness.

Doctor Franz shrugged, and turning, led the way. "He's in bad shape," he said, as he pushed open the door and stood aside for his visitor. "But I'm near certain he'll live."

The stranger halted on the threshold, scowling at the bandaged face in the low glow of a lamp. He turned on the doctor then. "It's Joel Harris I meant. Tell me, what's become of him—quick!"

The doctor had his turn for astonishment. "You mean you don't know that?" Then sudden realization struck him. "You're Wade Emery! But Mallard's men said you were dead!"

"They probably figured I was!" the other told him. "I woke up about an hour ago, on the floor of Harris's shack where they left me. Last thing I remember before that was hearing Bar M plot how they were going to take over Kingdom range—"

"We'd better do some talking," grunted the doctor. "Come back in the kitchen while we're at it, and let me take a look at that hole in your side."

Wade Emery's expression grew harder and more grim with every word of the doctor's recital. "Steve Mallard's running wild!" he exclaimed, once. That was when he heard of the murder of Dick Rudebaugh. And when he learned the plight of Joel Harris and Lynne Kingdom, he came driving to his feet with savage energy, shoving aside the little doctor who had removed the bloody bandage from his bullet wound.

"Sit down!" ordered Doctor Franz, crisply. "I'm not through with you!"

Emery obeyed, hardly knowing why. There was something about this thin, blue-eyed man with the scraggly muttonchop whiskers—a firmness of character oddly at variance with all he had heard of Terry Franz's drunken father. He wondered at this, as he let the man work at him with swift, sure fingers.

But then other concerns crowded these thoughts from him, and as soon as the doctor completed his inspection and straightened with a satisfied grunt, Emery was already coming to his feet, one hand reaching for the hat on the post of the chair. "Don't let anyone know I've been here, Doc," he grunted. "If Mallard thinks I'm dead, it will be better to let him go on thinking it a while!"

"But what do you imagine you can do, single-handed? Not a man will lift a finger against

Bar M! Everyone is scared to death—and waiting for the outcome of that siege in the courthouse!"

"How do I know what I'm going to do?" growled Wade Emery, savagely and tiredly. He left those words behind him as he shouldered through the screen door, and the faint coolness of the dark received him.

The voice of the doctor rose behind him, frightened but resolute: "Wait a minute! Maybe I can find a gun and—"

Emery did not wait, because he knew the little man could be of no help in a thing like this. He strode on to where he had left the grey snubbed to a picket of the back fence, and finding stirrup stepped up into leather.

At a slow walk he rode through the night, not admitting to himself the keen sense of futility that came over him. Presently the river showed at one hand and the trees of the little park stood motionless about him. He swung down in the shadow of the bandstand, stood with conflicting, hopeless plans swirling in his mind as he looked toward the big square of the courthouse bulking at the top of the grassy hill.

Light showed behind the bars of the second-story windows. There, he knew, Joel and Lynne Kingdom were holding out in their siege that had Steve Mallard stalemated. Doctor Franz had given him the picture; of Bar M men keeping constant guard against the prisoners breaking free, while over at the Clover Leaf their boss made his headquarters, waiting with his crew, in mounting impatience, for the imprisoned pair to cave. So far, even after a full day of suffocating heat and with no food or water reaching them, there had been no word of surrender from Joel and the Kingdom girl. And in the Blue Chip, Thad Kingdom would be sitting, deserted and alone, drinking steadily, waiting out the slow course of events.

Somehow, Wade Emery had to break open that pattern, somehow get aid to the two in the cellblock. He knew that, and he knew he would have to do it alone and against the full weight of Mallard's forces. It would be suicide to brace the Bar M owner, surrounded by his gunfighters in the saloon across from the courthouse. But there was Joel—If, some way, he could get to his friend, their two guns together would halve the desperate odds.

Across dry, clipped grass, Emery moved beneath the trees of the park and came up toward the rear of the ugly wooden structure.

There would be a trapdoor under that wooden cupola, he thought. If he could get up there, that would let him into the store rooms of the third floor, and so down the stairs to Joel. But climbing to the cupola was out of the question. Only one way left, then—the obvious, seemingly fatal. But because Mallard's gunfighters were not expecting

216

any help to come from outside to the besieged prisoners, it would be a chance. And since it was the only one, Wade Emery accepted it.

He went quietly up the steps to the rear door of the building. It stood open, to let in the night air, and he could look straight down the throat of the lamplit corridor toward the black gap of the front entrance, and the lights across the street. Three men were in the hallway. They had brought out a table and were seated around it playing poker for cartridges, their chairs placed so that they all could keep a constant eye on the narrow stairs winding up toward the gloom of the second story. The guns of all three guards lay on the table, ready to their hands. But one of them sat with his back to the open door, and that narrowed the odds a trifle.

Emery came into the doorway with his own gun in his fingers. He made no sound, yet the two facing him saw and at once cards dropped from their hands as they grabbed for tabled six-shooters. Emery dropped one before the man could get his weapon into line; the other sent a bullet over, wild, and then took Emery's lead and slid heavily sidewards off his chair.

The third man tangled with his chair legs, trying to get around to face the intruder. Through swirling powdersmoke he stared then, eyes rounding. "Emery!" He formed the name with trembling lips, and after that Wade Emery was upon him and blued gunbarrel laid across his skull stretched the man out in the litter of cards and bright cartridges, upon the table top.

To the booming echo of the shots, Emery yelled up the narrow stairs. "Joel! If you can make it, get down here! Quick!" Shouts were riding the still night air now, doors banging and feet pounding the street—Bar M gunfighters, heading for the confusion of gunfire that had broken loose in the sprawling courthouse. And there was another sound—the clang of steel as the cellblock door swung open, and then Joel's voice calling his name.

Wade Emery called back and started running forward, toward the open street door. Through it he saw the black shapes of men suddenly hit the broad wooden steps to the veranda, and he put two shots through and saw those steps instantly cleared. A lamp in a wall bracket gave the only light in the hallway, targeting him, and quickly he reached and turned down the wick. Even as the flame guttered out he sighted Joel Harris's gaunt face upon the stairs, and behind him Lynne Kingdom. Then they were coming through the darkness, Joel at a hobbling run.

"Get back, Lynne!" Wade Emery cried. Then, as the form of Joel Harris neared: "All right, Joel?"

"All right, Wade!" The man's voice sounded thick, with fatigue and thirst and hunger. "And I got a gun—"

"Then use it! Stand here at the door and keep that Bar M crew busy, and give me five minutes!"

"Where are you going?"

Emery answered: "After Steve Mallard. If I can drop him, the rest of them will quit!"

The other's anxious voice went with him as he turned quickly toward the open door. Out there in the dust, dark shapes moved—running men, and horses stomping and pitching at the tie-racks. The batwings of the Clover Leaf were swinging, Bar M men pouring out into the night; but after that first rush toward the courthouse steps there had only been confusion, and uncertainty. In a moment, Emery knew, someone would think to circle toward the back and the two in the dark hallway would be trapped. He must make his play before that moment came.

He went through the door at a low crouch, moving sidewards into the piled shadows of the veranda. Gunflame met him; he triggered at the flashes, and then Joel Harris's weapon started speaking in the dark opening behind him and at his accurate shooting the men out in the street fell back, seeking cover. The firing ceased. The scream of a frightened horse shrilled across the dust and a man's voice cursed monotonously. With the shock of gunfire making a numbness in his ears, Emery crossed the veranda and went over the rail, landing on the ground below with a solid jar that wakened the hurt of his bulletgouted side and made him halt a moment, shoulders back against the planks of the veranda facing, while a sudden dizzy spinning of the ground resolved itself.

Then he saw Steve Mallard, silhouetted against the lights of the Clover Leaf, and with no more compunction than he would have felt in shooting a mad dog Wade Emery lined down on him. It was a ridiculously easy shot. The trigger bit into his finger, tripped—but there was only the faint click of the hammer on a spent shell.

At the same instant Mallard shifted out of line and Emery cursed silently, knowing he had missed his chance because, for once, he had failed to count his shots. But mingled with the chagrin was something else—a kind of satisfaction. To have shot Mallard down, offhand, would not have been quite what he wanted, after all.

Now the Bar M boss was calling, across the tense stillness. "Harris—if it's you! Let's call quits to this foolishness and make a deal."

From the darkness of the hallway, Joel's answer came in a voice that was hoarse but steady enough. He told Mallard where he could go and what he could do with his deal, and the spirit behind the words touched Emery with cold humour as he broke open his six-gun, began jacking out the empty shells. The beginning of a smile died on his lips as he put a hand down toward his cartridge belt and found there only empty loops, and three lone cartridges.

He hesitated, fingering those three shells, and something close to despair rose within him. Three bullets. It was long since he had had the money to spare for ammunition, but he had not realized until this moment how low his stores had fallen.

Ross Boyden sang out: "Harris ain't alone over there, Steve. I saw another gun flash. There's at least one other siding him."

The sound of that voice reminded Emery of other things—of a fist smashing into his face, and of boots slogging his downed shape into unconsciousness. He remembered a promise he had made himself: that he would someday kill Ross Boyden. Bitter, that he could not keep that promise; because three bullets were just not enough, not against such odds.

A frightened horse reared, at the watering trough before the courthouse. In lamplight falling across the street, Wade Emery recognized Boyden's mount, and it was then he recalled a stolen rifle; a delicate instrument with telescopic sights and a trigger action like the smooth function of a human thought. He saw it thrust from the boot of Ross Boyden's saddle, and almost without thinking he came from the shadows and was under the hitchpole, into the deep dust and lifting that rifle from its holder.

It came into his hands with the feel of familiarity—and Wade Emery was a master with any weapon that he had ever once handled. He checked it briefly, found the cool metallic roundness of cartridges in the clip, and levered one quickly into place under the bolt. And then, with the stock of Joel Harris's rifle pressed into his hip, left hand forward about the barrel, he came out of the shadows, out of the drifting dust around the hitchrail, clear into the centre of the street.

"It's Wade Emery!" he called. "I'm coming for you, Mallard. And for Boyden, too."

Stunned silence met his words. Facing forward, Emery saw the dark cluster of men on the steps of the Clover Leaf. He saw that clot split apart, suddenly, and then only two standing elbow to elbow, as if frozen by their own astonishment. It was Ross Boyden that caved first, for he found himself suddenly in the very position he had so long dreaded—across sights from the gunslick of Saddleback. If he had been a coward he would have turned and bolted for the swinging doors at his back; but he was not a coward. So instead, he tried to throw a hasty bullet over before Wade Emery expected it. Only the bullet was a shade too hurried—and it was just the move Wade Emery had been looking for.

The rifle lashed into the boom of the six-gun, and Boyden's broad shape was falling. Emery, spread-eagled in the street, took the pound of the rifle against a braced thigh, and his stiffened left forearm forced the muzzle back into line as he pivoted slightly, toward Steve Mallard. Mallard shot then. He did not miss. The shock of the lead struck square and drove Wade Emery heavily to the ground, to his knees. He would have gone prone but caught his weight upon the butt of the rifle and leaned against it a moment, head hanging. Then, with all his strength, he pushed against that braced stock and got shakily onto his knees. His left arm hung useless, as though not a part of him. But, one-handed, he got the rifle up against his shoulder and the muzzle wavered into line.

There was no question of aiming, for he could not have held a bead that way and, in the moonlight, gunsights were useless things. He fired as he always did, by instinct. And then the recoil of the weapon was toppling him, and he slewed forward into the dust.

CHAPTER XVIII

There was a confusion of men in the big bar-room of the Blue Chip, but they stayed clear of the chair where Wade Emery had been placed by those who carried him in. Buck saw to that, and he saw to it that someone was sent hurrying for Doc Franz. And he brought a damp cloth and with awkward care swabbed the hurt man's face with it, so that presently the coolness of it worked through the fog of pain and Emery lifted his sagging head, stared about him uncomprehending.

"Here you are, mister!" Buck lifted a glass of whisky, and Emery swallowed it obediently. It cleared his brain, so that the world stopped spinning and the splintered lights hurting his eyes resolved themselves into shapes and colours. The face of the barkeeper came clear, and the contours of the room and of the table against which he sagged weakly. There was something else, too—the dull localized agony centering in a useless left arm.

Buck told him: "A clean break, I figure. Doc will slap some splints on it and the fin will be as good as ever, one of these days. Just sit easy until he gets here."

The other nodded heavily. After the hell of the last days, even this sort of peace was vaguely pleasant and he felt no impulse to stir, to break through the lethargy that held him. He was hardly aware of the excitement of men in the big room, and sounds came faintly. Even Buck's voice hardly registered as he said: "Here's something Terry Franz said to give you. She's been keeping it since last night, when she found it at the sheriff's house. Like everyone else, of course, she figured you was dead."

Then Buck moved away, and Emery tilted his head stiffly to look at the square of yellow paper that the bartender had left spread out before him on the table top. He stared at it for moments, foolishly; and only after the second reading did the meaning of the telegram pierce to his mind. But then he sat up with a sudden movement, reaching for the paper. He did not pick it up, but let it lie there while the words swam and took focus and stunned his bullet-shocked brain with their import:

"THIS OFFICE TRYING SIX
MONTHS CONTACT MAN KNOWN
TO YOU AS WADE EMERY STOP
PLEASE INFORM HIM CHARGES
HERE DROPPED FOLLOWING
CONFESSION OF PERJURY BY CHIEF
WITNESS IN CASE AGAINST HIM—"

Somewhere near at hand, someone laughed shortly, harshly. He realized it was himself, laughing at the ironic humour of this thing; at himself, chased by shadows through these long grim months on the back trails. Running from—nothing! Any other feelings were momentarily smothered under the heavy blanket of irony, and by the weariness that fogged his whole being.

. . . He awoke with the morning sun across his pillow, and lay for some minutes in puzzlement. He remembered then walking on his own two legs from the Blue Chip to the hotel, the hurt arm freshly bandaged, and climbing the stairs to this room, and collapsing upon the bed. Now the soft turning of the door's knob had wakened him, and long habit made him reach for a gun that he failed to find. But next moment the door had swung wide and Joel Harris looked in at him.

Joel's sombre mouth cracked into a smile as he saw his friend awake and heard his greeting, and he came in closing the door behind him. He moved with a limp as he crossed to the bed, but otherwise he seemed to have shaped up well enough after his ordeal. He said: "How do you feel?"

"Good enough," said Emery. "A night's rest can work magic with a man."

The other echoed: "A night's rest? Why you've been in that bed near thirty-six hours—never stirred once!"

Emery frowned. "Then no wonder I'm hungry!" He threw aside the sheet and light blanket, and despite his friend's protest got both legs over the side of the bed and both feet upon the carpet. A moment's weakness passed, and he could feel the strength surging through his rested body.

Sun and blue sky filled the window, above the fronts of the buildings across the street. A breeze stirred the cheap curtains. A clock in the watchmaker's shop next door sounded nine strokes. "Yes," grunted Emery, "I'm ready to go again!"

Joel leaned against the ironwork at the foot of the bed. "Everyone knows now about you," he said, slowly, "and about the answer to Rudebaugh's telegram. You'll be heading home, I guess?"

"I dunno. Not to more gunwork, at any rate. I've done a lot of thinking; that's a good country back there, and there's a quarter section I'd sort of like to try my hand at working."

"Fine!" exclaimed Joel. "I'm glad to see you put your gun away, for good. There's better things for you than gunswift!"

"But I wouldn't want to leave you in a hole—"

"Don't think of that! I can handle my own problems. For one thing, Bart Yaeger's due to hang for the murder of Dick Rudebaugh and he's been doing a lot of talking that clears me of all suspicion on that Crown hold-up." He hesitated.

"I'd like to ask your advice, though, on the thing. You'll be square with me?"

"Of course!"

Suddenly Joel paced to the window, with that painful limp, and for a long moment gazed out at nothing. When he turned his dark face was troubled, uncertain. He blurted then: "Have I a right to ask Terry Franz to marry me?"

"Terry—?" Wade looked his astonishment. "Well, she loves you. Or did you know?"

Joel nodded sombrely. "Yes, I—guessed as much. But—" He dropped his glance to the injured knee. "This leg will never amount to a great deal. Doc told me. And I got nothing to offer her but a two-bit mountain spread and the promise of back-breaking work." He shrugged, heavily. "The thing is, we're pretty much two of a kind, she and I. We've been kicked around, and had all the dirty breaks, and we've both been outcasts. We should be able to understand each other."

Wade Emery thought about this. He said, finally: "There were her brother and sister, and her dad. Something seems to have changed Doc Franz, and straightened him out—so perhaps now she can lay down that burden. But—she wouldn't want you, Joel, on a basis of pity!"

"It wouldn't be pity," said Joel, quickly.

Wade looked at him, dreading a subject that had to be put forward. "What about—Lynne Kingdom?"

Harris shook his head. "*That,* I think was pity. Or at the most, sympathy and friendship. Lynne could never be for me. She lives in sunshine, and would never understand my bitterness and my moods. Besides, with her I'm sure it's someone else."

"Someone else?" Wade Emery felt the touch of chill, and cursed himself for letting this affect him. But it must have shown in his face, for a twist of amusement lifted the corner of Joel Harris's mouth.

"Why, of course. You should have seen her sitting here by your bed hours on end while you were sleeping, half-crazy with worry until Doc convinced her you weren't in any danger!" He left these astonishing words behind him as he turned suddenly and moved towards the hall door, opened it. From there he swung back to indicate a bundle on the dressing table. "By the way, there's some new clothes she asked to have sent up. And a razor." He added, in a quick change of subject: "I'll order some breakfast, shall I?"

Wade Emery gestured with his good hand. He said on a dull tone: "No need to. I'm getting up!"

He shaved in the cracked mirror, his mind full of Joel's last astonishing words. The man was wrong, of course—dead wrong. Wade unrolled the bundle of clothes and looked at them for a long moment. His own were blood caked and ruined, and in the end he had no choice although taking these made him frown darkly with chagrin and hurt pride. He got into them awkwardly, working one-handed, and letting the sleeve of the new shirt ride empty above his broken arm. His strength, he found, had completely returned; he thought that now he was even able to ride.

He went down the dark stairs to the dining room, for he was ravenously hungry. But there were only a few coins in his pocket and he told the girl who came for his order: "I'll have to ask you first to put this on my bill." He had a full breakfast, then, sitting alone in the room with its white-draped tables, with the hum of a fly against the window pane.

His outward manner gave no hint of the inner turmoil of his thoughts. He seemed quite sure of himself as he rose and went out to the lobby and approached the desk. "I'm no deadbeat," he told the clerk, evenly, "but I've not got the money to pay for my meals and bed. I'll try to make some arrangement!"

But what the smiling clerk said then staggered him. "Your money is no good here, Mr. Emery. And the bill has already been settled. Incidentally," he added, lowering his voice with a conspiratorial wink, "someone out on the veranda will be most happy to see you!"

Wade Emery knew who it was, even before he turned and strode to the door and out upon the shaded porch, and saw Lynne Kingdom and her father. The girl gave a little gasp and came to him at once. She had never looked lovelier in her dainty riding habit and with the dark curls swept back from a face flushed with pleasure. The things she had endured seemed to have left no mark upon her. It was Thad Kingdom who had changed. He sat hunched over in a chair by the rail, and his ramrod back had rounded and his face was sunken and he was old—old now in spirit as well as body. But his eye held the same malignant spark of fire that had always been there. Nothing, it seemed, could damp that.

Lynne was at Emery's side now, and she placed a hand upon his unhurt arm and lifted her eyes to him in a look that brought back Joel Harris's words. But Wade Emery turned from her eyes, and he brushed aside the anxious questions she stammered. Face cold, he said crisply: "Miss Kingdom, I suppose I owe you thanks for taking care of my finances. You realized, of course, that I was broke. But I'm not for sale, to anyone. I assure you that someday I'll send you every penny that I owe you and your father!"

She stared at him, on a quickly indrawn breath. Suddenly unsure, she cried: "But you owe us nothing. It's we who—" She hesitated, his last words striking home suddenly. "*Send* us? You're leaving?"

"At once."

"But wait—please!" She had his arm again, and he let her lead him to her father's chair. Thad Kingdom sat there, unspeaking, his eyes watching the other sharply from behind drooping, blue-veined lids. Said Lynne: "Dad—that is, we—want you to stay, Wade Emery. We need you! Crown is in ashes, and you're the only hope of rebuilding it to what it was!"

"No, thanks!" Wade Emery's voice was like a whiplash, and it put new looks on the faces of both father and daughter. "I'd rather dig in the dirt of my own quarter-section, and never have a dime, than to grow rich with Thad Kingdom! His empire was built on greed, and cunning, and selfishness. And those things brought its ruin and left you both without friends or sympathy. He is no better than Steve Mallard was. I can't even blame Mallard for hating Crown—not when Thad Kingdom would have seen Mallard's range burn to cinders before lifting a finger to help in the disaster that struck when that slide came down!"

Faces gone white, Lynne Kingdom had recoiled a step and drawn back toward her father's chair. As for old Thad, his bony hands tightened on the arms of it and he hoisted himself partway to his feet, only to fall back with a grunt while his eyes blazed with fury at Emery and words trembled on his sunken lips.

"How dare you say such things?" Lynne managed, the colour returning and heightened by quick anger.

"Because they're true," Wade Emery answered her, "and because you know they're true!" He reached suddenly and found her hand. She did not withdraw it, but it lay limp and cold in his. "I love you, Lynne!" he added, tensely. "You've guessed that. But I love you too much for this. I'd build Crown to the stars—if it were for you. But not for this man—not for the purposes to which he'd put it. I'm asking you to come away with me; to leave Crown and all it means, behind you!"

Tears shone in her brown eyes, suddenly. She shook her head, her hand still in Emery's. "You're cruel, Wade Emery! How could I leave my father, when he needs me—"

"He doesn't need you, or anyone!" he retorted, and could not keep the contempt from his voice. "Look at him—he's far from whipped! Oh, he'll build Crown again, singlehanded. He'll build it the same greedy, unscrupulous way he did before. But at least I'll have no hand in doing it!"

A choked cry broke from the old man's throat. "Get out of here! I'll listen to no more of your insults!" His clawlike hand came up, trembling with rage.

And Wade Emery stepped back, his eyes and mouth hard. He looked at father and daughter, and he bowed a little and dragged on his battered hat. "Good-bye, then," he murmured. "I'd like to wish you both and Crown good luck, but I can't bring myself to do it!"

Nor could he bring himself to look squarely at Lynne Kingdom before turning on his heel and striding away down the steps of the hotel. His last picture of her was as she stood beside her father's chair, the stubbornness of her jaw breaking against the hurt of her brown eyes. He shut the picture from him deliberately, and the lines of his lean face were hard as he went toward the livery barn to find his horse.

One of the last things he had found strength to do that night, after the shooting, was to ask that the grey be returned to its owner, and his own jughead roan be located and put into a stall at the livery. It was there now, the patched saddle and harness hanging beside it, and it shook out its mane in greeting as Wade Emery came into the straw-strewn corridor. He slapped the neck of the ugly bronc, and he called the hostler.

It was the same here as at the hotel. The Kingdoms had settled in advance for the stall and the feed, and Wade Emery shrugged as he heard this. He had done more than enough for the Kingdoms, he thought. It was only fitting they should do this much in return. But he would pay back every cent, would admit of no indebtedness to Crown.

With his hurt arm, he had to have help in

putting on the blanket and saddle. Then he swung up and the saddle felt familiar and good beneath him as he rode out of the coolness of the barn and into the beginning heat of the day.

He knew many feelings as he rode through this town for the last time, but regret was not one of them. Not regret for the way he had broken with the Kingdoms. There was honour, and there was self-respect, and these things a man could not sacrifice forever. Even love, sometimes, came too high at that price. And he had no reason now to think that Lynne Kingdom had ever loved him—that she had not merely been playing her father's game of intrigue and cunning, to win his services for the betterment of Crown. She was Thad Kingdom's daughter, he knew, in more ways than one.

The last buildings dropped behind, and there was the tawny trail ahead, and at the top of a knoll, a vantage point from which he could see the range spread out behind him. He reined up here, and turned, and had his look. Tree-heads dropped dustily above the street where he had killed men—for the Kingdoms, he thought once more, bitterly. And there was the park, and the river and the courthouse with the pigeons circling. There, too, were the hills and the deep, wide pass of the Saddle. He looked at it all for the last time.

And then he turned away, and there was Lynne Kingdom on the back of Prince, waiting.

"Lynne?" he exclaimed, astonishment in him.

She told him, in a quick rush of speech: "When you left us, father talked. He cursed you, in the foulest language I had ever heard from any man. He had no gratitude for all you had done. He was only thinking of the future—of Crown—of what he would do to climb to the same heights he reached before. He—" The hurried voice broke suddenly, and the brown head bowed forward. "Without intending, he showed me the kind of man he really is—just the kind you said, and that I always knew he was, but never had the courage to admit it to myself!"

There seemed nothing to say. Wade Emery reached with his good hand and covered the fingers that were tight upon her saddlehorn, and then let the hand drop away again. She raised her head then, and her eyes were dry and her jaw determined. "I won't throw myself at your head!" she declared, fiercely. "But if you'll still have me—I want to go with you. I want no more of Crown, or the name of Kingdom, or what they stand for. I'd rather dig in the dirt, as you say—and hold my head high!"

Wade Emery smiled then, and there was no bitterness or uncertainty in him now. "Perhaps," he said, "it won't be as hard as that. What do you say—shall we just ride ahead, and see where the trail takes us?"

"Yes," breathed Lynne, and found an answering smile. "Wherever the trail takes us. You point the way!"

Center Point Large Print
600 Brooks Road / PO Box 1
Thorndike, ME 04986-0001 USA

(207) 568-3717

**US & Canada:
1 800 929-9108**
www.centerpointlargeprint.com